dark secret

FRANK MURPHY

THE O'BRIEN PRESS
DUBLIN

First published 2000 by The O'Brien Press Ltd.,
20 Victoria Road, Dublin 6, Ireland.
Tel. +353 1 4923333; Fax. +353 1 4922777
E-mail books@obrien.ie
Website www.obrien.ie

ISBN: 0-86278-678-9

British Library Cataloguing-in-Publication Data
Murphy, Frank
Dark Secret
1.Children's stories
I.Title
823.9'14[J]

1 2 3 4 5 6 7 8 9 10
00 01 02 03 04 05 06 07

The O'Brien Press receives
assistance from

The Arts Council
An Chomhairle Ealaíon

Editing, typesetting, ayout and design: The O'Brien Press Ltd.
Colour Separations: C&A Print Services Ltd.
Printing: Guernsey Press

DARK SECRET

FRANK MURPHY

Having worked as a school principal, and written poetry, school books and short stories in his spare time, Frank wrote his first novel for children, *Lockie and Dadge*, when he retired. It went on to win a Bisto Book of the Year Merit Award and the Eilís Dillon Memorial Award. He is also the author of *Charlie Harte and his Two-wheeled Tiger*, and a book for younger readers, *The Big Fight*, which is a retelling of the classic saga, *The Táin*.

CONTENTS

Dedication

My thanks are due to those kind friends who read an early draft of this story: Anne Coleman, Pat Egan, Ted and Fiona Garvey, Marie Morgan, Joe O'Donoghue, Tim O'Mahony.

A special word of thanks for the children of the Swan School and thier teacher, John Cotter, and also for the children of fifth class in Scoil Ában Naofa, Baile Bhúirne, and their teacher, Stiana Ó Céilleachair.

Bernie O'Sullivan told me about sheep, and Bill Downey put me wise on the ways of the countryside and especially on how to tickle a trout.

1

David, the Bedrock

David felt the sunlight falling warm on his closed eyelids. He still had his clothes on, but he was cold as a frozen snowball from lying outside the bedclothes. He had been up until after midnight, waiting for his dad to come home. But when tiredness fogged his eyes, he had thrown himself on the bed, and collapsed into a nightmare.

About an hour later, he had come half-awake at the sound of someone stumbling over furniture downstairs. Then a voice cursed a chair for being in the wrong place, and he knew Dad was home, so he went back to the world of his troubled dreams.

It was the sound of traffic that woke him in the morning. Cars were growling out of the estate, backing up at the intersection with the main road. The tailback was as far as Branagans' house, number two, three doors down from their own. So it was past eight o'clock. The milk van pulled up outside the door, and that settled it. You could set your clock by the milkman.

Time to get up. Get ready for school. He didn't have to because who cared? Not his dad anyway. But he had promised *her* that he'd be good. He would go to school every day, and 'make something of himself', *her* words. He stepped across the landing to the bathroom and washed. Back in the bedroom he pulled on his shirt. It wasn't spotlessly clean, the way *she* would have had it. But she didn't get a chance to show him how to work the washing machine in those last few weeks before she was taken to hospital. His last sight of her was scorched on his memory.

She lay on the stretcher, and kept looking up at the window, her eyes locked on his until the door of the ambulance closed.

His dad flipped when she died. Now he spent almost every night in Mulhall's pub, so David had no one to talk to. 'You'll have to be strong,' she had said to him. 'And help your dad.'

Wasn't it strange that she should have said that? How could he be the bedrock when he was only thirteen years old? 'You're a lot like my own dad,' she had said, 'as solid as a rock. As hard to move too.'

David didn't feel solid now, just heart-sore and very mixed up. Why did it have to be himself and his dad? They were gutted, while the rest of the world just carried on as if nothing had happened. But he had to be brave, like she had been. It didn't matter how much it hurt, he mustn't show it. Nobody must know that the tears were dammed up behind his eyes, waiting to spill out.

The only way to deal with that was to put it behind him, out of his mind. That's what she would have done. He mustn't think about her. Too painful! She's gone and that's that! Nothing to do now but get on with it. Then was then. Now is now.

In the next room his dad was lying on his back, his face red, his mouth open, breathing like someone at the end of a race. The window had been closed all night and the air in the room was warm and stale with the smell of beer. David looked at his dad and he wanted to shout in anger; how had the bright, laughing, joking dad he had known all his life changed into this semiconscious wretch?

But both of them couldn't opt out. One of them had to keep the ship afloat, and right now it had to be David.

'Dad?' David tried to wake the sleeper. He called a few times but he might as well have been shouting at a stone wall. David had to shake him. The man in the bed struggled out of his heavy sleep and opened his eyes, looking at David as if he had forgotten who he was.

'Wh-what is it?' he stammered.

'Time to be out of there,' David said. 'It's after eight.'

'Oh no!' Dad moaned. 'I feel like a sick horse.'

David went downstairs and got his breakfast – cornflakes and bread and butter. That was the last of the food. He went upstairs again.

'Dad, you'll be late for work,' he said.

'OK. Phone them for me and tell them I'm sick.'

'That's three times in two weeks.'

Silence.

'I need some money,' David said.

'For what?'

'There's nothing to eat.'

'Take it out of my pocket,' Dad said and he turned away and pulled the bedclothes up over his head.

Dad's pants were thrown on the floor. David took the wallet from the back pocket. There were only two notes in it, a ten and a twenty, and David took the ten.

At lunchtime he sat staring at his maths book because he had nothing else to do. All around him, in the normal world, he could hear them crunching crisps or biting into apples.

Susan Branagan's voice cut in on his thoughts. 'I can't eat all these sandwiches, David,' she said. 'You want some?'

'It's OK,' David said, ashamed.

'Pity to throw them in the bin,' Susan said. 'They're nice sandwiches, but I've got too many.'

'It's OK. I'm not hungry,' David said, but his mouth watered at the thought of sinking his teeth into a sandwich. He could feel his face turn red. He turned around and faced Susan, 'Anyway, I don't want your leftovers.'

Susan looked at him, her eyes like saucers.

'Sorry, Sue,' David blurted out. 'I didn't mean that. But I'm OK. Honest.'

That wasn't fair to Sue, and he knew it. Sue was cool! He'd been walking around in a daze for weeks, and ever since he'd stopped hanging around with his usual gang, she'd been the only person in the school who'd talk to him. But that didn't matter. He didn't want her sympathy, or anyone's sympathy. In the end though, she didn't throw the sandwiches into the bin. She managed to eat them all.

✝   ✝   ✝

Back home in the evening, David looked around the kitchen and decided he really had to catch a hold of things. If he didn't, the place would turn into a slum. His dad was on another plane for the time being, so it was up to him. He washed clothes and ironed shirts, and made out a timetable for doing the housework. It was hard work, but at least it kept his mind occupied.

His dad didn't notice the clean-up when he came in that night, or, if he did, he didn't say anything about it. He was still going around spaced out. A few days later he came home and announced that he wouldn't be going to work any more. They had fired him. David was in the kitchen and Dad came in, faced the cooker, and began making wild accusations, blaming everyone and everything but himself.

'Can you believe it?' he roared. 'Eighteen years slaving for that shower, and this is my thanks.'

David just listened, not knowing what to say. Dad took a can of beer from the fridge and opened it. He tilted it to his mouth, and David watched his Adam's apple moving up and down as he guzzled the whole can without a pause. Then they both just stood in silence, neither one wanting to catch the other's eye.

'What's your next move, Dad?' David asked eventually.

'Don't know. Look for another job I suppose.'

He sat down, and looked over at David for a while. Then tears welled in his eyes. 'I haven't been fair to you, David,' he said. 'I'm sorry. You've had to do the housework and everything.'

'That's OK,' David said slowly. 'You've had a hard time.'

'And what about you? Wasn't she your mother?' David heard the tears in his voice, and he hoped that getting fired would make his dad face up to what had happened. David himself had faced up to it, but only on the outside. His mind was a dark room of despair.

2

Dreaming of Sheep

Dad was never without a glass in his hand, or a can of beer. David was constantly removing cans from the table, chairs, windowsills, and picking them off the floor. The house began to smell like a brewery.

One day he came home and couldn't open the back door. Something was blocking it. He pushed and pushed until he forced it back to make a gap large enough for him to squeeze through.

It was his dad, lying helpless just inside the door. David fell on his knees beside him and shook him, screaming, 'Dad! Dad!' But there was no answer. David thought he might be dead. He jumped to his feet and charged out of the house.

He found himself at Branagan's door, his finger on the bell and he could hear it ringing, ringing, non-stop.

'Hello, David,' Mrs Branagan said, but then she saw the panic in the boy's eyes. 'Something wrong?' she asked.

What followed would be forever a confused jumble in his memory. The ambulance, the stretcher; following the ambulance in Mrs Branagan's car; sitting with her in the hospital waiting room; going back to the Branagans' house and staying there for the night. Then the relief when word came from the hospital that his dad would be OK, although it would take some time.

✢ ✢ ✢

Back in the Regional Hospital his dad looked fine.

'They want me to go to another hospital for a while,' he said to David.

'But you're not sick, are you?'

'No. Just a bit broken up,' Dad said. 'We'll be back together as soon as I get out.

'I can go to see you, can't I?'

'It's a different kind of hospital they have in mind.'

'You're an alcoholic, isn't that it?' David said. His tone was vicious. He was attacking his father.

'Oh God, David, do you have to say it out like that?'

'There's no point in fooling around.'

Dad saw David's anxious face. 'No need for you to worry,' he said. 'I'll be home in no time.'

In the meantime, where was David going to live? He wanted to go home, but the social worker who came from the hospital that morning would have none of it. He heard the words 'into care' and Mrs Branagan saying, 'He'll stay with us, of course.' Mrs Branagan was a bossy kind of woman. She got on the phone to her husband and before long they had it all fixed up: David was going to stay with the Branagans until his dad came home.

The Branagans did everything in their power to make David feel at home. Mrs Branagan was a busy woman, with three children of her own, but she fussed over him like a hen with a chick. She seemed to be constantly hovering in the background, checking up on him. No doubt she could see, from his dark look and his blank, unsmiling face, that he was dejected.

'I'm going up to number five to check it out, David,' she said one afternoon. 'Would you like to come with me?'

'Am – ah,' David hesitated. 'I must sweep the driveway for Mr Branagan.' He found it too hard even to look at his real home.

'The driveway can wait,' Mrs Branagan said, and David couldn't think of a good reason to refuse. The woman had good intentions, but she hadn't a clue. Did she think going back to his home would cheer him up or something?

✢   ✢   ✢

Mrs Branagan opened the door. They went into the silent house. David was shocked by the smell – musty, like a squat. The house had taken on a different life, and felt alien to him.

Mrs Branagan went into every room and cast an eye around. When she skipped upstairs, David moped into the living-room. He stood in the centre of the room and forced himself to look. The clock on the mantelpiece had stopped. The figurine of the ballet dancer beside it still stood poised on one toe. The fisherman in the watercolour over the fireplace stood by the reedy pool, his line still in the air in an extravagant loop as he cast it far out over the water.

All the old things lay where they had always lain, like dead souls in some kind of limbo, waiting for the sound of remembered voices, the warm touch of familiar hands, to bring them back to life.

David looked at the photos standing on the sideboard. It was like coming to a family gathering. One photo showed the three of them, himself in his confirmation suit, his mom and his dad, smiling as if tomorrow would be as good as today. Two grandmothers and one grandfather looked out at him, unsmiling. They had already gone to another kind of tomorrow. Mom's father wasn't there, the old man David had seen at her funeral. Mom used to go to see him once every month, but David and Dad never went.

'Let's give him a miss,' Dad would say.

Other than his dad, that old man was the only relative David had in Ireland. All he knew about his grandfather was that his name was Batt Quilty, and he was a sheep farmer in Knocklee above the valley of Glenfune, almost ten miles from Coombowler in Kerry.

David tried to picture him, to summon up his image and give him his rightful position with the others on the sideboard. He recalled the elderly man moving ahead of him in the funeral procession. He had worn a grey-green tweed jacket. Then there was his grey hair, cropped short, and David remembered above all else his silence.

Nobody spoke to the man, nor did he try to speak to anyone. Like a silent vessel moving in a convoy, he was among them, shipping his own cargo of thoughts, his own grief. David tried to put himself in his place. He must have been heartbroken too. This old man was part of David's past, even though they had never spoken to each other. They had a shared past in a way. It didn't matter that they had occupied different patches of space on the planet – they were of one blood. And then David remembered his mother saying to him, 'You're a lot like my own dad …'

'Well, that's it. Everything is fine.' Mrs Branagan broke in on his thoughts.

'Did you get the smell?' David asked.

'Yes, it's a bit musty. You get that when a place isn't lived in. You must come up now and then and open the windows to give the place an airing.'

David found it hard to go to sleep that night. He tried to count sheep, but every time he imagined them skipping through a gap, there was his grandfather, leaning on a shepherd's crook, watching the creatures go past. It didn't matter which way he turned, he couldn't banish the image from his mind, and it was the last thing he saw with his inner eye as he dropped down into sleep. Again and again throughout the next day the same image swam into his mind.

3

To Coombowler on the Bus

'We're getting holidays on Friday week,' Susan told her mother when they came in from school one day.

'Good!' Mrs Branagan said. 'We're off to Spain on the following Monday.'

'You never said!' Susan said accusingly.

'I know. I wanted to be sure Dad could get away, and no hitches. We're taking a villa this time, in Andalusia.'

Mrs Branagan turned to David. 'What about you, David? Do you think you'll like it?'

'Oh!' David exclaimed. 'Am I going too?'

'Of course you are,' Mrs Branagan was emphatic. 'You don't think we'd leave you here on your own.'

That night, David lay on his bed, wide awake, for a long time. He couldn't shake the image from his mind of an old man in a grey-green tweed jacket.

'No time better than now,' he said to himself as he sat up, pulled on his slippers and crept down the stairs. A line of light under the door of the den told him that Mr Branagan was there.

'Come in,' Mr Branagan called when David knocked.

'What is it, David?' Mr Branagan raised his eyebrows, obviously surprised to see David there at that hour.

'Have you time to talk to me?' David asked.

'Yes, come in. Tell me what's been worrying you,' he said.

'It's about going to Spain,' David said.

'You're coming with us of course,' Mr Branagan said, as if to reassure David that he was included in their plans.

'I don't want you to think that I wouldn't like to go,' David said, 'but there's somewhere else I'd like to go more.'

'Oh! And where is that?'

David told him that he wanted to visit his grandfather.

Mr Branagan didn't say anything for a while, just took his pen and tapped it on the desk.

'Look, David,' he said. 'I'll talk about it to Jo, and I'll make a few enquiries. We'll see.'

✛ ✛ ✛

'We're thinking of letting you go to see your grandad,' Mrs Branagan said two days later. 'Matt looked into it and we're happy about it.'

Mr Branagan was a lawyer and he had got in touch with a colleague, a Mr John Falvey in the town of Coombowler. Not alone did Mr Falvey know David's grandfather, Batt Quilty, but Mr Quilty was one of Falvey's clients. He praised the old man, and thought it would be fine for David to spend time with him. He also suggested that Batt Quilty might enjoy the company.

So it was all arranged. David would go on the bus to Coombowler on Sunday, and his grandfather would meet him there. When the Branagans returned from Spain, they would go to Knocklee to bring him back.

At the bus station Sue and Jackie said, 'Bye, David. We'll send you a card from Spain.'

Mrs Branagan kissed him, and he was surprised and embarrassed to see tears in her eyes.

Mr Branagan had given David forty pounds – 'for your ticket and any other expenses'. Mrs Branagan had slipped him a ten-pound note in the bus station, so he was loaded, even when he had paid the five pounds for his ticket.

As the bus moved through the green countryside and put

miles between them and the city, David couldn't put it out of his head that he was moving into a different life. He felt as though he could breathe more freely already, looking out over the fields and trees. He wondered how he would cope 'in the wilds', as Sue called it. It was exciting, even if it was only for a few weeks.

The bus slowed as it moved into the outskirts of Coombowler, and then crawled through a long, wide street, with just a few cars parked nose to kerb. They pulled up at a bar that carried a bus stop sign over its door. The driver announced a ten-minute break, and all but a few women and one old man shuffled out of the bus.

David looked around to find his grandfather, but he wasn't there. There was nothing for him to do but wait by the door of the bar until the old man turned up.

Fifteen minutes later the bus passengers came straggling back to their seats. It had been parked there for fully twenty minutes before it moved off, throwing back a jet of grey exhaust fumes as if to mock the boy standing forlorn at the door of the bar.

David stepped out into the middle of the road and looked right and left. There was no sign of his grandfather. Perhaps he was in the bar, and didn't know that the bus had come. David went in. Two men sat on high stools at the counter, and the barman was moving among tables, laying beer mats on them. He looked up when David entered.

'Well, boy,' he said. 'What do you want?'

'I'm looking for my grandfather,' David told him, determined to remain calm.

'And who's your grandfather?'

David told them.

'Knocklee?' the barman said, and he scratched his head. 'Do

you know where Knocklee is, Bill?' he asked one of the men at the counter.

'It's out beyond the village of Tubber,' the man said. 'It's up Glenfune way, about three miles from Tubber.'

'A lot of sheep out that way,' his companion said.

'That's where your man lives,' Bill said, his voice lowered to share a confidence, but David heard him well enough.

'Who?' Bill's companion asked, also keeping his voice down.

'Don't you remember? A good few years ago now,' and he whispered something in his friend's ear.

The companion's eyes lit up in sudden recollection.

'Oh, yes,' he said, and the two of them stared at him, curious, as if they'd like to ask him a question.

'Would you show me the way?' David said.

'How are you travelling?' the man, Bill, asked.

'I'm walking.'

'That's a long way to walk, boy,' the man said. 'Five miles to Tubber, and another three miles from there. That'll take you a while.'

'I'll try to thumb a lift,' David said.

Bill came to the door with David and showed him the road to Knocklee. David thanked him and took the first steps on the long walk to the home of his mother's people.

4

Batt Andy

David left the empty streets of the town and walked along a quiet road between fences crowned with whitethorn bushes. Nearly two weary hours later, tired feet brought him to Tubber. It wasn't really a village, just two houses, a church and a school. One of the houses was a shop and also the local post office. There wasn't a soul on the road. The houses looked very cosy and inviting, and the blue light of a television set flickered in one of the windows. David kept walking.

After Tubber the sky darkened and a drizzle came down, a cool blanket of small raindrops. Then, at the bottom of a slope, a signpost to Glenfune pointed to a road leading east through a gap in low hills. It was more a lane than a road. Beyond the gap the landscape opened out, and David found himself in a glen, a huge saucer completely enclosed in its circle of hills and cut off from the rest of the world.

'Where are you going to, young fellow?' a voice behind him made him jump. It was a rough-looking woman with a head of hair like a furze bush, beaded in raindrops, and wearing thick trousers stuffed into wellingtons. She must have come over the roadside fence.

'To Knocklee,' David said when he had recovered from his shock. 'Do you know where it is?'

'It's about half a mile up the glen,' she said. 'Are you going to Batt Andy's?'

'To Batt Quilty.'

'The same man.' The woman stood looking at him for a long time, examining his face as if she could read some story there.

'You must be Tessa's boy,' she said eventually.

'I am.'

'And you lost her, I heard. I'm sorry for your trouble, boy. What's your own name?'

'David.'

'You're not afraid to be going up there?' the woman asked, fixing him with a steady gaze.

'No. Should I be?'

'No, no! It's just that Batt Andy keeps to himself a lot.' She turned to a frail-looking man who had come out of the house nearby. 'Pete, will you go along with this young lad and show him Batt Andy's place? David, if you're ever scared or if you need help, come down here to us. My name is Mary Murdon, and that's Pete. Your mother was in my class in school, and we were good friends.'

For a minute her words about being scared made David think of turning back, but he didn't fancy going straight back to Branagans' and telling them that he had changed his mind. Besides, it was starting to get dark. He wondered what she meant about being scared. Was she just trying to frighten him? Whatever it was, she didn't seem to like his grandfather.

As they walked along, Pete kept saying to himself, 'Batt Andy's. Batt Andy's!' David walked a couple of paces behind.

They came to a lane leading up to a ridge that looked like an outpost for the hill. The only indication that there was a house there was a thread of light blue smoke curling above the ridge and fading from sight against the background of grey stone that mottled the hillside.

Pete pointed at the smoke and said, 'Batt Andy's!' and he laughed.

21

'Thanks,' David said, and he walked up the lane. It wasn't paved, just a wide path of gravelly earth between stone fences, with a light cover of grass. When he crossed over the crest of the ridge, David saw a two-storey stone house standing on its own in a grassy hollow. The far side of the hollow rose to become part of the steep slope of the stony hillside. A line of sheds, built of the same type of stone, stood about twenty metres from the house. Two goats nibbled at the short grass near the sheds.

A man, the man he had seen at his mother's funeral, was bolting the door of one of the sheds. He stopped and slowly turned around. He looked up for a few seconds at David. Then he turned his head away and went to the goats. He released the animals from chains that tethered them to an iron spike driven into the ground. Then he went into the house.

David didn't know what to do. This was not a good beginning. Did his grandfather not want to know him? Maybe he thought David was a stranger, and maybe he didn't like strangers. David had no other option but to go down and introduce himself.

He knocked at the door, but got no answer. He knocked again, louder.

'Come in,' a deep voice called.

David raised the latch and walked into a kitchen that was also a living room. A fire burned in a range and on it a kettle and a large pot shot out jets of steam. His grandfather raised the pot cover and tried a spoonful of its contents for taste. He was wearing a heavy, sleeveless cardigan, and a striped shirt without a collar.

'You came,' he said simply.

The old man didn't turn around, but began to stir the pot. He went to the dresser, took down two large plates and laid them on the table. He lifted the pot off the range and brought it to the table, tilted the pot and poured out a brown stew, some into both plates. He went to a fridge in the corner and took out a glass jug of milk. He poured milk into one of the mugs, but hesitated before pouring some into the other one.

'Do you drink goat's milk?' he asked without looking at David.

'I've never drunk it before,' David said.

'Want to try it?'

'I don't think so.'

Batt took a tumbler from the dresser and went to a white bucket on a stand beside the sink. He filled the tumbler with water from the bucket and placed it on the table for David.

'Why didn't you take the water from the tap?' David asked.

'This is spring water from the well at the back.'

'Why?'

'Why what?'

'Why go to the bother of bringing in a bucket of water when you have it there in the tap?'

'The well water is good.'

'Isn't it all water?'

''Tis, but different.'

'So what's so good about the well water?'

'The well water is cool and clear and pure because it comes from deep in the ground. Eat.'

That put an end to the conversation, and they ate in silence. Then Batt stood up and took the plates to the sink. He emptied the remains of David's plate into a wide enamel dish, added a few potatoes in their skins and the rest of the stew from the pot.

'Here, take that out to Homer,' he said and handed the dish to David.

'Who's Homer?' David asked.

'The dog. Go out the back door. He's waiting for it.'

23

David went out, and, as soon as he appeared, a black and white collie rushed at him, barking and snarling. David was afraid of him for a moment, but when the dog saw the dish he stopped and began to wag his tail. David put the dish on the ground and Homer attacked the food as if he hadn't seen a bite in days.

'Now he knows who you are,' Batt said. 'He's a cute old fellow. Knows better than to bite the hand that feeds him.'

5

Davy

David watched Batt as the old man stood at the sink, washing up. He held the dishes gingerly in his large hands and placed each one so gently on the draining board that they hardly made a sound. David listened to the silence – there wasn't a sound in the house but the rattle of dishes and the lapping of water in the sink. He could even hear Homer chomping on his food outside the back door.

'Grandad?' David began cautiously.

His grandfather grunted in reply.

'Why didn't you turn up in Coombowler to meet me?' David asked.

'I thought you weren't coming until next Sunday. And call me Batt.'

'How did you get the days mixed up?' David whinged.

'John Falvey said the third,' he said.

'And what date do you think this is?' David asked, still cranky.

'I don't keep track of dates,' Batt said.

'You didn't ask me why I came,' David said. He felt like shouting.

'I was hoping you might tell me.'

Silence descended again, and again it was David who broke it.

'Can I stay here for a few weeks?'

'I don't know,' Batt said as he passed over and back from sink to dresser, putting the dishes back on the shelves. When everything had been put away, he went to the table and sat down opposite David.

'You have a story for me, boy?' he said.

His eyes were grey-blue and bright, and so steady that David knew he would listen to what he had to say. He poured out the story of his troubles – his father's problems, the Branagans, the social worker, his wish to come to Knocklee, the bus journey, and the long walk from Coombowler.

The old man listened in total silence. When David finished, he sat for a while, thinking.

'You can stay,' he said at last.

Then he stood up and, without another word, moved ponderously to the stairs. All his movements were slow and deliberate, like a man who cherished the time he was given to do what he had to do. David stayed at the table, wondering what was next on the programme. The sound of Batt moving from room to room on the bare boards overhead kept him guessing. Then the footsteps moved to the head of the stairs, and the voice called, 'Davy'.

David shot out of the chair, shocked. That name, 'Davy'! His mother used to call him 'Davy', but no one else. He stood, unable to move, as a stream of memories like old snapshots shuffled across his mind. He had to block them out because they brought with them too much pain.

'Are you there?' his grandfather called.

'I'm coming,' David answered, raising his voice in a show of annoyance.

Upstairs he was shown his room, a room at the front of the house with a view down the glen. David looked out the window. He could see the Murdon house and another derelict house nearer, and a house at the other side of the glen road.

When they came downstairs, Batt invited David to go for a walk
with him.

'If you're not too tired after your long walk today.'

David said he wasn't tired at all, and they went out. David
asked why they didn't lock the door as they left.

'Nobody locks a door around here,' Batt said.

He showed David the sheds. The last in line was a garage. It
had no door, only three walls and a corrugated tin roof. An old
Ford Escort was inside, dark brown on top and fawn below. It
was so old it must have been vintage. The tool shed had a chain
and padlock.

'Why do you lock the shed if you don't lock the house?' David
asked.

'That's another story,' he was told, and David felt that he was
being kept at arms' length. They walked the short distance to
the top of the ridge in front of the house.

'I call this the rampart,' Batt said, stamping his foot on the
ground. They could see most of the glen from there, a private
kind of place bordered by its own hills, with its own road and,
overhead, its own circle of sky. It was so open and so free, David
thought, so different from the city where he had been surrounded by houses and people.

The Quilty land stretched from the roadside to the top of the
hill. It was bounded on the west side by Murdons' farm, and on
the east by 'a place owned by German people'.

'Whose house is that?' David asked, pointing at the ruin that
stood between their own place and the Murdons'. Its windows
were smashed, and black holes here and there in the roof
showed where slates were missing.

'It's Murdons' now. It used to be Tim Heffernan's. They
called him "Tim the Fiddler". His land was divided between us

27

and the Murdons when the old fellow died, because he had no living relative to claim it. I didn't want the house, so the Murdons took it, and that took some neck.'

'Why?'

'Never mind.'

Again David felt he was being pushed aside.

✛ ✛ ✛

Before they went to bed, Batt said, 'We'll say a prayer before we go.' He put his elbows on the table, cupped his face in his hands, and slowly recited the twenty-third psalm:

> *The Lord is my shepherd; I shall not want.*
> *He maketh me to lie down in green pastures:*
> *He leadeth me beside the still waters ...*

It wasn't anything like the prayers David was used to. Was it a prayer at all? Surely, in a prayer one had to ask for something.

'That's not a proper prayer!' he said arrogantly.

'Isn't it?' Batt said. 'So what is it then?'

'I don't know what it is,' David said disparagingly. 'Sounds like some weirdo sheep saying nice things about the shepherd.'

Batt just moved about, stowing things away in the press and the dresser drawers, until the room was shipshape.

'And what are those wacko words about?' David persisted. 'Couldn't they say it plain?'

'What do you mean "wacko"?'

'Words like "maketh" and "leadeth" and "preparest". Words like that are weird.'

'They're the words, boy, and it wouldn't be right to change them.'

'What would be wrong with changing them?'

''Twouldn't be the same. They're the words they've always been. I say them every night, and if you are going to be staying here for a while, you'll be saying them with me.'

'I don't know them,' David said.

'Well then,' said Batt patiently, 'just listen to them until you do know them, and when you do we'll be saying them together.'

David had to admit to himself that the ancient words fitted in with the whole scene, a glen that had been left behind by the march of time.

But he still hadn't forgiven his grandfather for making him walk all the way from Coombowler.

Once David had closed his eyes, there was no sound to wake him until he heard Batt downstairs the following morning. In the kitchen the table was laid for two, and Batt was cutting brown bread. The kettle was steaming on the range, a porridge pot was bubbling, and two fish sizzled on a frying pan.

Batt turned the fish, saying, 'Nice and fresh, these lads. Caught them in the night lines.'

'In the what?' David asked.

'Night lines. I'll show you soon. In the meantime have a look around for yourself for a few days. See what kind of a place you're in.'

David took him at his word and spent the next few days exploring. He examined the farm buildings, the tractor and trailer and the ancient Ford Escort. A large turf rick and a stack of new hay bales stood in the place Batt called the 'haggard'. At one end stood a huge standing stone, like a gravestone, but rough and much bigger. David examined it and saw strange designs cut into its face, cups surrounded by circles. Their edges were blurred by the wind and weather of centuries. It stood upright like an ancient sentinel, as if to say, 'This place has a history'.

'That gallaun was stood there by the people that went before us in ancient times,' Batt said. 'I don't know why they put it there. Maybe 'twas the first Quilty marking his claim to this hill.'

✠ ✠ ✠

David quickly settled into the pace of life on Batt's farm. There was time to think in a place like this, and he felt that he had room to breathe. He loved being able to look into the distance and watch the weather coming long before it arrived in the glen.

A fenced-in paddock behind the house was called the 'sheepfold', and at one end of it was the dipping pond.

Batt explained, 'The sheep are dipped there: we push them into a concoction to keep off ticks and crawlies of all kinds.'

There was also a vegetable garden, with carrots, parsnips and such, fenced off to stop the goats getting in.

But David's main interest was the stream that flowed out of a lake near the top of the hill. He went along by the bank and climbed up to the lake. Its still water was backed by a sheer cliff, a wall of dark bare rock. Above the lake a few sheep quietly grazed on a stretch of green, heather-clad pasture. David couldn't see a way up, and he wondered how the sheep got there.

'You have to go around the back of the hill,' Batt told him later. The stream was the beginning of the Glenfune River, he said, and the lake was known as Doolough.

'That means the black lake,' Batt said.

'Why is the water so black looking?' David asked.

'Water has no colour, boy,' Batt said. 'What you're looking at is the reflection of the cliff.'

6

On Top of the World

'Come up the hill with me today,' Batt said one morning.

'What for?' David asked.

'Because 'tis a fine day and I'm going up to have a look. You might as well come along.'

'Have a look at what?'

'Dad blast it man, you take nothing for granted, do you?'

'Not like you.'

'What do you mean?'

'You take everything for granted, me especially.'

'You're as spiky as a ball of thorny wire, boy,' Batt said, and he laughed. 'All I want is to get you to know the place.'

'Sorry,' David apologised. He was doing that all the time, flaring up and then feeling sorry.

'And besides.'

'What?'

'It's beautiful up there on a day like this. Well worth the climb. You can see into four or five counties on a clear day.'

Batt brought sandwiches and bottles of spring water in a satchel that he carried over one shoulder. A pair of binoculars was slung from his neck and rested on his chest.

'Put on your boots,' he told David.

'I haven't any.'

'No boots? Well, the weather is good and the place is dry. Those plasticky things will do well enough.'

The first part of the journey was easy and David had no trouble in keeping up with Batt, but when they got on to the steeper slopes, he was short of breath and fell further and further behind. Batt charged up the slopes, leaning forward and striding like a mountain goat. He waited for David at a level spot.

'You'll have to get into training, boy,' he said when David arrived, panting.

'How do you do it?' David asked, amazed at the old man. 'You were almost running.'

'Practice. There's nearly fifty years training behind me. We'll take it slower from here.'

Sheep looked up from their grazing when the humans invaded their patch. David was surprised to see some of them edge up to Batt and stand still while he fondled their heads and scratched their ears, as you would a dog. He bent down and spoke to them, softly, a soothing murmur. Then the sheep went back to their quiet browsing, nibbling at the short grass and heather.

David followed Batt around the west side of the hill. When they got to the top, David stood and drew in great mouthfuls of heather-scented air. He stood high above the valley, in a clean, clear world close to the sky. His troubles and cares seemed not to matter so much up there. He would be happy to stay all day on top of that hill.

They sat down on the grass and ate the sandwiches, washing them down with the spring water. Batt looked through the binoculars, turning slowly to take in the entire hilltop and much of the slope on the south side.

'What are you looking at?' David asked.

'Just checking on the sheep.'

'Are they OK?'

'They are, but one of them might be in a bit of bother on the other side of the lake.'

32

'What kind of bother?' David asked.

'We'll go down that way and you'll see.'

David was getting to know his grandfather; a miser with words. He didn't use two words where one would do, but what he said, he meant. He said David would see on the way down, so he would see. To tell him first and then let him see for himself would be redundant.

They examined the wire fence at the northern boundary of the farm. Then they walked over to look at the boundary with Murdons' farm, a large-mesh wire fence stretching from the top of the hill right down to the glen road.

'Why is the ground so bare on that side?' David asked.

'Overgrazing.'

'And look at the sheep,' David went on. 'They're all so miserable and scrawny.'

'Hungry!'

'How come?'

'One thing is the cause of the other.'

'But – but–'

'Work it out for yourself. Ah, there she is,' Batt said, and he pointed to where a sheep lay on its back, its legs sticking straight up. Batt clutched fistfuls of wool on the animal's side and heaved it upright. It trotted away and stood looking at them for a few seconds, then turned its back and began to graze.

'The sheep must be the most stupid creature in the world,' Batt said.

'Why do you say that?'

'I don't know of any other animal that doesn't know how to get up when it falls down.'

As they were going down the hill, David was thinking about the poor state of Murdons' land and their miserable sheep.

'Why do Murdons keep too many sheep?' he asked.

Batt laughed. 'Ah!' The penny dropped,' he said. 'I wouldn't be too hard on the Murdons. Who knows what pressures other people have?'

✛ ✛ ✛

They had left the lake behind and continued on down the hill by the bank of a stream. Batt stopped at a place where the slope levelled out and the water slowed to form a little pool. He examined the pool for a moment before continuing down the slope. He stopped again at the next pool and stood gazing into it for a long time.

'I think this might be the place,' he said. 'Take off your shoes and we'll cross the stream.'

'What are we doing now?' David asked.

'We might be able to catch a trout.'

'How can you catch a trout? You haven't a rod or a net or anything,' David said.

'If there's a trout there, I can try to tickle it.'

David laughed. 'You're having me on!'

'Come on and watch.'

'No, I'll stay here. I'll go across when I hear it laughing.'

Batt took off boots and socks and left them on the bank. He stepped into the water where it hurried over a gravel bed beyond the still pool. He waded across the stream to the opposite bank.

'Stay still there,' he called. 'Don't be moving around.'

David sat down and watched. The bank at the other side overhung the water by a foot or so. Batt removed his jacket and rolled his shirtsleeve right up to his shoulder. He lay face down on the bank and reached towards the water.

'Don't move now,' he said in a whisper. 'They get frightened if they spot anything moving above them.'

David couldn't believe that anyone could move so slowly. At

first Batt just touched the surface of the water with his finger-tips. They seemed to rest there for ages, but then David noticed that they had already entered the water up to the first finger joints. He didn't see the fingers move but gradually they slid deeper and deeper until all the hand was under the surface.

Slowly, ever slowly, the hand was lowered, and the water came up over the wrist, then higher, almost to the elbow. Batt's eyes were closed, all his attention focused on his task.

Then, without warning, the hand shot out of the water, scattering a shower of drops into the air. Something left Batt's hand, flew past David's ear and landed on the grass behind him. He turned and saw a fish, its dark, stippled body wriggling and flapping. Batt came back across the stream and took the fish. He put his finger under the gill and raised his capture.

'A tidy little fellow,' he said. 'Will go nice with your tea.'

David thought it was beautiful, with its dark, torpedo-like body and its silvery underside. Its tail was still flapping back and forth, but gradually it stopped. Batt pulled up some long grass and wrapped the trout in it and put it in his satchel.

'You must show me how to do that,' David said as they headed for the house.

'I will. 'Tis all in the touch.'

'The touch?'

'Yes. Gentle. Not to frighten.'

7

A Tumult of Squeals

The glen was a haven of quiet. One day followed another and David didn't speak a word to a human being other than Batt. He saw people move around the house at the other side of the glen road, but they were too far away for him to even know what they looked like. So, one morning when the green post van topped the rampart and rolled forward to the house, he stood stock still and fastened his eyes on it until it pulled up beside him. The door opened and the postman slid to the ground. He stood there, a tall man with a black postage stamp of a moustache under his nose, and held a letter aloft like a prize.

'Who are you?' he asked David.

David told him.

'You must be Tessa's boy?'

'That's right,' David said sullenly. Why did people have to say her name all the time?

'Poor Tessa! A letter for you.'

He handed David the letter, got back into the van and turned it in a wide circle. As he passed David on the way out, he lowered the window and called, 'From the city. Posted yesterday.'

The letter was from Sue Branagan:

Dear David,

We're back from Spain. We had a marvellous time. How was it with you? Mam told me to write to you to let you know that we'll go down to bring you home next

Sunday. I'll keep all the news about the holiday until we see you, and you can tell us what it was like out there in the wilds.

Your fond friend,
Susan

PS. Why doesn't your grandad get a phone?

David had asked him about a phone, but he dismissed the idea: 'I like to look a person in the face when I talk to them. How can I know how he's taking it if I'm talking to him through a wire?'

David had forgotten all about going back to the Branagans. In three short weeks he had settled into life in Knocklee, become part of the place as if he had been there his whole life. He slipped into his grandfather's routine – feeding the dog, digging potatoes and carrots for the dinner, going up the hill with Batt to check the sheep, finding the goats and bringing them into the haggard to be milked, going out early in the morning to check the night lines, doing things around the house, sweeping, washing up.

He showed Batt the letter.

'That's fine,' Batt said. 'You'll be glad to get back to civilisation.'

David said nothing. He should have had a hundred and one reasons to be glad to be going back to civilisation, but he wasn't too sure about that. Why was he not really delighted to be going back to the city? Was it that he didn't want to be depending again on the Branagans' charity? But, if that was the case, what about Batt's charity?

Well, that was different. Batt was family. And you didn't even have to say 'thanks'. Not to Batt. He wouldn't see the need to be thanked. But there was more to it than that. Back in the city he would be an exile once more in the house of the Branagans, and only a few steps away from his own home.

David spent most of the days and parts of the nights from then until Sunday wrestling with the big decision he had to make. Would he ask Batt to let him stay on in Knocklee until the end of the summer holidays? Would Batt agree? Would the Branagans be offended? Should he ask Batt now and write to Sue, to save them the bother of coming down?

✜ ✜ ✜

Sunday came and David still hadn't made up his mind. He and Batt spent the morning preparing dinner.

'Why are you going to so much trouble?' David asked.

'We may be in the wilds, as that young lady wrote to you, but we must let them see that we're half tame ourselves. And besides, they were good enough to take you in when you had nowhere to go.'

David didn't expect Batt to think of things like that.

The Branagans arrived close to noon. They came in a tumult of squeals of delight by the children and more restrained greetings from the parents, but all of them were broad-faced with smiles, and looking tanned and relaxed after their holiday. David introduced them to Batt and he shook their hands soberly.

Mr Branagan said, 'It was very kind of you to have David while we were away.'

'Why wouldn't I have him?' Batt said, and David thought it might have sounded curt to the others, but he knew that Batt didn't mean it like that.

'We brought you something,' Sue said to David.

It was a red T-shirt with a bullfighter in a typical bullfighter pose – standing stiff, head inclined, and holding his cape to tempt the bull to charge.

'We brought you something too,' Mr Branagan said to Batt.

He gave him a small plastic bag. Batt took out a package and opened it. It contained a Swiss army knife, with all the implements – blades, corkscrew, can opener, spoon, file, screwdriver and so on.

Batt held it in his hand, speechless. He looked at the knife and then at Mr and Mrs Branagan.

'Thanks,' he said eventually, 'but why?'

Mrs Branagan smiled, obviously surprised at Batt's reaction.

'Oh, I don't know,' she said. 'We thought you might find it useful.'

Batt looked at the knife again, then at Mrs Branagan. He was obviously not used to getting presents. For one moment, he was like a small child, looking up shyly at the Branagans.

'Thanks,' he said again.

The uncomfortable silence that followed was broken by Mr Branagan suggesting that David could show the children around the farm. He and Mrs Branagan would stay and have a few words with Batt. David would have given the crown jewels to know what those words might be.

'Fine,' Batt said. 'The dinner will be ready in about an hour.'

David brought Sue and young Jackie and Mattie on a tour of the sheds, the sheepfold, the dipping trough. He pointed to where the lake was and they saw its water spilling out as a small waterfall below it. Sue wanted to go up to see the lake, but David said it would take too long to go up and come down again. They walked along the bank of the river. From a fuschia bush David took two wooden pegs with fishing lines wound on them.

'They're night lines,' he explained. 'We put worms on the hooks and we drive the pegs into the ground. Then we let the lines into the river and leave them there for the night. Most mornings when we check them out, we have a trout or two for breakfast.'

They heard Batt calling them, and they ran back to the house.

All through the meal Sue and Jackie kept up a constant chatter about Spain and their holiday.

'You would have loved it,' Sue said to David.

'It wasn't so bad here,' David said, and out of the corner of his eye he saw Batt raise his head and look in his direction.

'Many sheep over there?' Batt asked. It was his only contribution to the conversation.

'Well,' Mr Branagan said, 'we didn't see any. We just flew straight to Almeria airport, and the journey to Mojacar was through semi-desert. Not a place for sheep. But I'm told they have a lot of sheep on the high lands, in the Basque country and places like that.'

'Can I ask something?' David said timidly in a lull in the talk.

Batt nodded.

'Would it be OK if I stayed here for another while, until the end of the holidays, sort of?'

Nobody spoke for a while.

'Are you sure that's what you want to do?' Mrs Branagan asked.

Before David could answer, Mr Branagan said, 'I don't know if it would be OK, David. Strictly speaking there is an obligation on us to remain responsible for you until your father can take over again.'

'I've been here three weeks,' David said. 'And I'm not dead yet.'

'David,' Sue said, 'this place is miles away from everything.'

'It's away from some things,' David said, 'but it's nearer to other things.'

If they had asked him to say what things were nearer, he wouldn't have been able to answer, but he knew deep in his soul that there was something on that hillside that the city didn't have.

Mrs Branagan was gazing steadily at David, and her eyes had gone shiny. 'If his grandfather has no objection,' she said quietly, 'I think he should be allowed to stay.'

'It's not that simple —' her husband began to say, but she interrupted.

'Oh, please Matt,' she said, 'don't annoy us with all those old legal "cans" and "can'ts". Why can't he stay here if he wants to?'

'His father might not want that.'

'His father is out of the scene now. It's up to us to decide what's best. Anyway, I think he should be told the truth about his father.'

David's ears pricked up at that.

'Well, what is best for him?' Mr Branagan asked, hurrying his words as if he didn't want the truth about David's father to come out.

'To be here with his grandfather is what's best for him, if that's what he wants,' Mrs Branagan said.

'We haven't asked Mr Quilty what he feels about it.'

'He can stay here for as long as he likes,' Batt said.

And so it was decided. Mrs Branagan, aided by Batt, persuaded Mr Branagan that, whatever the legal position, David should stay with Batt until the end of the holidays.

'What is the truth about my dad that I should know?' David asked.

Batt and Mr Branagan sat dumb, but Mrs Branagan spoke.

'He left the hospital and went to England, David' she said. 'He discharged himself, and they couldn't hold him.'

'Where is he now?' David asked anxiously.

'We don't know. He hasn't been in touch.'

'He'll get in touch when he's ready,' David said. 'I know he will.'

8

I'm Not Homer

Next morning Batt came out of the bathroom, shaved and spruce-looking, but for a tiny scrap of newspaper sticking to his chin.

'I have to go into Coombowler today,' he told David. 'I think you should come with me.'

'Why?'

'We have to do a few things.'

'Like what?'

'Like get you a strong pair of boots for the hill if you're going to be here for another five or six weeks.'

After breakfast they set out for Coombowler in the old Ford Escort, travelling at twenty-five miles an hour. Neither of them spoke until they left the byroad at Tubber and moved on to the wide main road between Abbeydare and Coombowler. The pace didn't change.

'Can it go faster?' David asked.

'It can.'

'Why don't you?'

'What?'

'Go faster.'

'No reason. I like this speed. Comfortable.'

The topic of speed was exhausted. They eased into Coombowler, past the fancy new houses with lawns and flowers, and David broke the silence for a second time.

'Is that all we're coming in for, to buy me boots?' he asked.

'No. I want to see the solicitor as well.'

Batt parked the car and they walked up the main street. David wasn't sure if it was just his imagination, but one or two of the locals seemed to be watching Batt, and they whispered amongst each other when he passed. Batt walked past, with his head erect and his chin thrust out.

Their first attempt at shopping for boots for David was inglorious. The shop, Dardy's, was dingy, stuffed from floor to ceiling with men's, women's and children's clothing of every kind – tracksuits, football shorts, pinstripe suits, high fashion, everything. Batt baulked at going in, but David saw 'mad' boots in the window.

The shopkeeper was a middle-aged man with a grey moustache. He was dressed like a tailor's dummy, in a dark suit, stark white shirt and dark blue tie.

'What do you want, Quilty?' he snarled.

Batt didn't answer, so David spoke: 'Boots,' he said. 'I saw a pair I might like in the window.'

The shopkeeper, who had been glaring at Batt as if he'd like to wither him, turned to David. 'If you're with Quilty,' he growled, 'we don't have your size.'

'It's all right, Davy,' Batt said. 'We'll get them somewhere else.'

He turned and walked out of the shop, and David followed.

'What was that about?' David asked when they were back on the street.

'Something before your time, boy. Don't let it bother you.'

The assistant in the next shop was a young man in shirtsleeves. He was eager to show them everything they had in the shop and they left carrying armfuls of parcels containing shirts, pants, jumpers, socks, pyjamas, boots, underwear, a heavy overcoat and an anorak.

'Why are you getting me all that stuff?' David asked. 'I have plenty clothes at home. They'll still be there when I get back.'

'No good at home if you wanted them here.'

'Anyway, what'll I be doing on the hill?' David asked.

'Helping me out with the sheep,' Batt said.

'There's more to it than that, isn't there?' David said. 'You're thinking I might stay on after the summer?'

'I can't tell the future, but sure, there's no harm in being ready for anything that might come up.'

'You think of everything,' David said.

'I try.'

'But what I think doesn't matter!'

Batt was silent for a minute.

'Sorry, Davy,' he said. 'So used to being on my own I forget I should talk about things.'

'My dad will come back you know,' said David.

'I know.'

✤ ✤ ✤

They put the parcels in the boot of the car, and then went to Wolfe Tone Street.

Mr Falvey, the solicitor, was a short, grey-haired man. He shook hands with Batt and nodded at David.

'And this must be young David Lakes,' he said.

'Yes,' replied Batt. 'It's about him I want to talk to you.'

Batt told David's story in very few words.

'Forgive me,' Mr Falvey said, 'but I'm not clear about a few things. Matt Branagan didn't give me a lot of details.'

He asked how the boy came to be with the Branagans. Was there any possibility of contacting his father?

'Why didn't his father contact you before he let him go to the Branagans?' he asked Batt.

'He wouldn't,' Batt said.

'But why not? It would be a natural thing for him to do, you'd think.'

'We weren't talking for a long time.'

'Oh. Did you have a fight?' Mr Falvey smiled.

'No.'

'I don't understand.'

'It was his doing. He didn't allow Davy to have anything to do with me.' Batt was matter-of-fact, no anger, no sadness.

'Why?'

'I don't know. Because of that bit of bother fifteen years ago, I suppose.'

'Oh, I see,' Mr Falvey said slowly. 'A bit unreasonable, I think. After all, you were cleared.'

'By the law I was.'

Mr Falvey scribbled a few notes on his pad.

'I don't think it's a problem,' he said. 'I'll write to Matt Branagan and tell him you wish to take temporary custody of the boy, until his father is well enough to look after him again. I doubt if he'll object to that. Strictly speaking he should consult the boy's father, but if the man's not available, that can't be done.'

'You don't think the past will come into it with Branagan?' Batt asked.

'No, Batt. The past is a clean slate, regardless of what a few oddities might wish to think.'

✢ ✢ ✢

As they walked back to the car, David said, 'I don't know where I am.'

'How so?'

'All this stuff is going on around me, and it's about me, and I don't know what it's all about. What's the dark secret?'

'What are you talking about?'

'Everything!' and he tried to mimic the people who had spoken. '"If you're with Quilty we haven't got your size!" "That little bit of bother fifteen years ago, I suppose!" "The past is a clean slate!"'

'Certain things you're better off not knowing.'

'Well, I have news for you, Grandad!' David raised his voice and emphasised the word 'Grandad', knowing that Batt didn't like to be called that. 'I'm me. I'm David Lakes. I'm not Homer. If you want to talk over my head, I haven't much business staying here. I might as well be back with the Branagans. At least they don't treat me like a bit of furniture.'

'No!' Batt shouted. 'You liked being with them so well that you didn't want to go back with them.'

He stopped shouting and spoke in a milder tone: 'Don't worry. If you want to go back, I won't stop you. They're good people and you'd be all right with them.'

'Well, they didn't shunt me around from Billy to Jack without telling me what it was all about.' David was still agitated and a few passers-by stood and watched.

'Is that old fellow giving you grief?' a hard-faced woman asked.

'You mind your own business,' David shouted at her.

Batt laughed. 'Come into the car and we'll talk,' he said.

They sat in and Batt started the engine and backed out. As they trundled along home, Batt said, 'You have a marvellous temper, boy. Are you always like that?'

David had calmed down. 'No. Not really. I'd just like to know what's going to happen to me, and I don't like people deciding things for me without talking to me about them.'

'All right, Davy. You'll have to take me as I am. I'm too long now making decisions without having to hold a meeting.'

The car chugged along at Batt's eccentric pace until they

came to the turn off into the Tubber Road. Batt slowed still more as they went over the bumpy road through the bog.

'You didn't mention your mother yet,' he said.

David didn't answer.

'Why?' Batt asked.

David took a while to reply. 'She's dead,' he said.

'I know.'

'She was my mother, the only one I had.'

'She was my daughter.'

'It's not the same thing.'

'I know, but close.'

Batt changed gear as they climbed a short rise.

'Don't worry, Davy, you'll be all right,' said Batt.

For the rest of the journey they didn't speak.

Meeting the Young Ones

*B*att didn't move with the times. If something was good enough, he didn't see a need to splash out money on improving it. David gradually came to terms with his antiquated way of doing things.

Monday was washday in Knocklee. Batt didn't have a washing machine, and he cleaned his clothes by boiling them. Shirts, underwear, socks, hankies, nightshirts, pyjamas were all thrown into a huge cauldron and boiled for hours.

'Boiling is the only thing,' he said. 'That's if you want to get them clean.'

David was given the job of keeping the clothes moving in the water by poking at them now and then with a flat board. The kitchen became like a sauna as the cauldron shot out jets of steam under its rattling cover. David had to add water from time to time, and then the steam thinned out until the cauldron reached boiling point again. Beads of water settled on the windowpanes, and on David's skin; he threw off his shirt.

One Monday, as he poked absentmindedly at the frothing mass of clothes and bubbling water, somebody knocked at the door. When David opened it, John Falvey, the solicitor from Coombowler, stood there, his mouth hanging open in amazement. He raised his briefcase to shield his face from a belch of warm fog that broke away from the main force swirling around the kitchen.

David had to step into the open to talk to him.

'What's going on?' Mr Favley asked.

'Nothing,' David said. 'Just washing clothes.'

'Oh!' Mr Falvey exclaimed. 'Is your grandfather around?'

'No. He's gone up the hill,' David told him.

'OK. I just felt like coming out for the spin. Tell him that I had a reply from Matt Branagan.'

He took a sheet of paper from the briefcase and handed it to David.

'That's a copy for him,' he said. 'Matt goes along with your staying here. He just asked me to remind your grandfather that you're due to start in secondary school this autumn. Tell Batt to call to my office next time he's in town.'

David was spreading the clothes on the furze bushes in the haggard when Batt got back from the hill. David told him about Mr Falvey's visit, and handed over the letter.

'You were talking to them about me staying longer than the summer, weren't you?' asked David, a note of annoyance in his voice.

'I was when they told me your father had skedaddled.'

'You can think what you like about him, but he's sound. You'll see, when he gets over his trouble he'll be back again.' David felt a surge of anger, and fought to control it.

Batt read the letter slowly, then folded it and went upstairs. David could hear the footsteps in the bedroom overhead. They stopped and, after a short pause, there was a scraping sound, as of a heavy box or chest being pulled across the timber floorboards. Silence then for a brief moment, then the same scraping sound as the box was pushed back to its original position.

'Under his bed,' David murmured to himself. He wondered what treasure or dark secrets were hidden there.

✢ ✢ ✢

The next day they went up the hill to bring the sheep down to be dipped. Homer did most of the work. Batt directed him with a stream of arcane shouts and whistles and a ballet of arm movements. The little black and white collie scampered here and there over the hillside, moving the black-faced sheep, until a large flock was gathered beside the lake. As they moved down the hillside, they were joined by strays coming unbidden from all sides.

Batt sent David ahead to open the gap in the sheepfold fence. But he didn't have to, because it had already been opened by Ned Farren, the thin, raw-boned farmer from across the glen. When he had seen the flock making its way down the hill, he knew the drill and came to help.

They spent the whole afternoon dipping the sheep. David and Homer hustled them one by one to the passage leading to the dipping trough. Ned took over there, forcing them along the passage and into the liquid filling the trough. Batt stood at the side, and, as each sheep sank into the bath, he placed a forked stick over the animal's neck and pushed down until the sheep was completely covered. When the sheep came out at the other end, it skirted the sheepfold, and they let it drift back up the hill.

'Thanks, Ned,' Batt said as his neighbour departed. 'I'll be over there about noon tomorrow.'

'Fine,' Ned said. 'Will you come too, Davy?'

'For what?'

Batt laughed. 'Don't mind him, Ned,' he said. 'Our Davy takes nothing for granted.' He turned to his grandson. 'Ned is dipping tomorrow, and we're giving him a hand,' he explained.

'Not so much to give a hand,' Ned said. 'We have plenty help, but he might like to meet the young ones.'

✛ ✛ ✛

David met 'the young ones' next day: four of them. Of the six children, the two eldest brothers had summer jobs in Coombowler. The youngest, Ruth, stood back from Batt and David, eyeing them shyly. A girl and a boy, Lucy and Teddy, were less bashful and came closer.

Batt gave them the usual stuff from grown-ups who hadn't a clue about young people: What's your name? Are you a good girl? Do you do jobs for your father and mother? How are you getting on at school? They gave him one-word answers, hung their heads, and moved timidly from foot to foot.

Farren's flock soon arrived, a choir of bleaters with dog barking solo bringing up the rear. The dog, Sayers, could have been Homer's twin. Ned was driving the sheep, and his helper was a girl about David's age. She wore jeans and a jumper that must have been her mother's. It hung loosely about her and came down almost to her knees. She ran ahead of the flock and guided them into a temporary enclosure bounded by bales of hay.

David joined her in driving the sheep to the dipping trough. It was exactly as it had been on Batt's farm, except that Batt urged the sheep into the trough and Ned pushed them under with the forked stick. As David and the girl worked, they had idle spells when a number of sheep were waiting in the passage leading to the trough. At first she was quiet and didn't talk, but as time went on she grew bolder.

'You're Davy Lakes,' she said. 'We heard about Tessa. We were very sorry for you.'

'What's your name?' David asked, as if she hadn't mentioned his mother.

'I'm Josie,' she said. 'Was it awful?'

'Was what awful?'

'Your mother dying. I didn't know you then, but I was lonesome thinking about it.'

'Haven't you anything else to talk about?' David asked, his

voice sharp with annoyance.

She blushed pink, and he noticed her oval face, like a picture he had seen of Mona Lisa. Then, as she turned away from him in embarrassment, he saw that her long black hair reached down to her waist.

'Sorry,' he said, and he hurried to the far side of the enclosure to round up a few sheep. He glanced towards Batt and Ned, and he saw that Batt was eyeing him from under his shaggy eyebrows. When they had finished, Ned and Batt piked the hay bales back to the rick in the haggard. Ned's wife came out, a dark woman with a peaceful face.

'Come in now; I have it ready,' she said.

'We're a great trouble to you,' Batt said.

'No trouble at all,' she said, and she turned to David. 'You must be Davy. How do you like the glen? I suppose you find it a big change from the city.'

'Yes, Mrs Farren,' David said, and he hoped she wouldn't start sympathising with him. She didn't.

'Call me Julie,' she said. 'I don't like Mr and Mrs. It's kind of, not friendly.'

They had a tasty salad, and the conversation turned to schooling.

'What class is Josie in now?' Batt asked.

'She's finished in Tubber school this year,' Julie said. 'Starting in the Community College in town after the holidays.'

'That's a good distance,' Batt said. 'Getting there will be awkward enough.'

'Won't she have the school bus,' Ned said. 'They'll walk out to the end of the road and the bus will pick them up and drop them back there again after school.'

'I forgot they have the bus,' Batt said. 'Not like our time, Ned. Davy will be starting off too, after the summer. They

52

might be going together.'

✛ ✛ ✛

As they walked home, David said: 'You're sure I'll be here in September? I might be going back to the Branagans.'

Batt just walked on, saying nothing.

'Well?' David persisted. 'What about that?'

Batt stopped and looked up at the top of Knocklee, thinking, as if he weren't sure whether he should say what he was going to say.

'I don't think you'll be going home, Davy, for a while anyway. The Branagans took you in because otherwise you'd have had to go into care. Now they think you belong here.'

'How do you know that?' David asked.

'They told me so the day they were here.'

That evening when David went to his bedroom, a framed photograph was standing on the locker beside his bed. It was a photograph of a girl, a girl with long hair like Josie Farren's. David stared at it, wondering who it was and why Batt had put it there. But gradually the features took on a familiar look, the bright eyes, like Batt's, with their heavy lids, the slim, arched eyebrows, the soft lips on the verge of a smile.

It was his mother, but she wasn't his mother then. It was Tessa, young and happy, not knowing how little time there lay ahead. She didn't know him then, nor he her. It was almost as if she were someone else. David felt a rush of anger tinged with sadness. He didn't want to think about her! He turned the picture face down on the locker and began to get ready for bed.

10

Exploring the Glen

The shearer spent most of a day's daylight wrestling sheep to the ground and running the shears all over them until he had stripped them of their wool. Then, looking like skinny dogs, they ran out of the shed and headed for the hill. At twilight he packed the fleeces into his van and drove off.

'Did you sell him all that wool?' David asked.

'In a way,' Batt said. 'The price of wool is very low. It barely covers the shearer's wage for doing the job.'

They applied for a place for David in the Community College in Coombowler for the coming school year. A week later the postman brought a letter offering David a place in the school and listing the things he should have on entry – the school uniform, football gear, track suit, and a lot of books. The shops selling the books and uniform were named.

They had no trouble with the books, but the school uniform was available only in Dardy's shop, the one that refused to sell David boots on his first visit there. Batt got around the problem with the help of Julie Farren. She had to get the girl's uniform for Josie, and she measured David and got a boy's uniform for him. The shopkeeper wanted to have him in to fit it, but she said, 'He's not with us at the moment,' and she got the clothes.

David began to visit the Farren home uninvited. If he happened to arrive at mealtime, he was given a place at the table and shared their food and their talk.

He explored the glen. Sometimes Josie and the two younger

children, Lucy and Teddy, acted as guides. They visited an old well that had a reputation for curing rheumatism, and they walked along the empty glen road, past Schaublins', the lone house owned by the Germans near the head of the glen, to reach a waterfall. The water fell from a great height, but in that dry summer it was only a trickle.

'You must come to see it in the winter,' Josie said. 'It's a mighty sight then.'

Josie was quiet and serious and didn't laugh much. But once she and David got to know each other, they prattled non-stop.

'I never saw your mother,' she said to him one day. 'What was she like?'

'She's gone,' he said, 'and I don't want to talk about it. What kind of a weird interest have you got in her?'

'Nothing,' Josie said. 'I just thought you might like to talk to me about her.'

'Why would I want to do that?'

'I don't know. You must be feeling sad, and I thought it might be good if you had someone to talk to about it.'

'You haven't a clue. You're for the birds!'

Josie blushed. 'Sorry!' she said.

'It's OK,' David tried at once to make up for his ill-mannered response to her kindness. 'It's just I can manage on my own.'

Josie didn't speak of his mother again.

One Sunday they decided to walk the three miles to Tubber to a football match. Josie and Teddy were with David.

'That was Tim the Fiddler's house,' Teddy said as they passed. 'He's dead.'

'He died a long time ago,' Josie said.

'How long?' David asked.

'I heard he died the week before I was born,' Josie said.

'Yeah,' David said. 'I heard his name.'

A little further on they came to Murdons' house. Pete was leaning on the gate.

'Hello,' he called to them, and his eyes followed them as they went by.

'Who's the fellow with the yellow shirt?' he shouted after them.

David was surprised. Could he have forgotten him so soon? He was the one who had shown him where Batt's house was when he first arrived in the glen.

'He's Davy Lakes,' Teddy shouted back at him. 'Batt Andy's his grandfather.'

'Ha-ha-ha!' Pete laughed. 'How's Batt Andy? How's Batt Andy? Ha-ha-ha!'

His sister, Mary, came out of the house and waved at them, then said something to Pete and he went indoors with her.

'Don't mind him,' Josie said. 'Some days he's not too with it. He forgets everything.'

✛ ✛ ✛

Knocklee had become David's new home, and calling it 'home' in his own mind had, in a way, blurred his ties with the home in the city. But he had to write to Sue, to let her know how he was faring. It wasn't right to break his ties with the Branagans. He would have phoned, but Batt didn't have a phone.

Dear Sue,

I'm starting in to Secondary School in the Community College in Coombowler after the summer. I don't know what it will be like, but a friend from the other side of the glen will be starting too. She's Josie Farren, and she has two sisters and three brothers. We'll be going in and out in the yellow bus.

I expect my dad won't be too long in England, and

he'll be bringing me back soon, but I like it here. Batt doesn't talk much, but he's OK, and he looks after the sheep well. I think that's good.

I help him around the farm, saving hay, bringing in the goats to be milked, feeding Homer the dog, digging the vegetables in the garden for the dinner, going up the hill to check out the sheep, and lots of other jobs. It's different and I like it.

Goodbye for now,
From,
David.

The day before he started in the Community College he got a reply:

Hi David,

I was delighted to get your letter. It was five weeks and four days from the time we saw you in Knocklee.

Your dad was back home for a weekend. We told him you were staying with your grandfather, and he wasn't too pleased about that. I don't think he likes your grandfather too much. He called him an old reprobate, whatever that is. Anyway, he said he would send for you when he came back. We are still minding the house.

We would like very much to go to see you, but Mam says we should wait until we're invited. I hope you'll invite us soon.

Bye for now,
Sue.

David thought about inviting them to Knocklee, but he didn't talk to Batt about it. He decided to wait a while. In a way he would be glad if it wasn't too soon. In Knocklee he was miles away from his old life, and that was OK.

11

Killer's Breed

The Community College opened on the first Wednesday in September.

'Are you sure you have everything?' Batt said.

'I'm sure.'

'I'll walk down to the end of the boreen with you.'

'You don't have to,' David said. 'I think I can make it that far.'

'I know,' Batt said, 'but it's your first day and all.'

'I was in school before, you know.'

'Are you frightened?'

'Frightened of what?'

'Nothing. You might be finding it a bit strange. And anyway, take no notice of them if they say things to you.'

David wondered why Batt was so uptight about his going to school.

'What things would they be saying to me?' he asked.

'I don't know,' Batt said. 'Those townies have suspicious minds and insulting tongues.'

'So what?' David laughed. 'You're forgetting that I'm a townie too.'

'Anyway, good luck go with you. It's a big day in your life.'

The Farrens had come out and were waiting for him by their gate. Eddie, who was a year older than Josie, was there too. He was going into third year.

'Hi, Davy,' he said. 'Your first day. It's OK. I'd say you'll like it.'

The first few weeks flew by. They got used to having seven different teachers, and soon learned their nicknames. David liked especially Starchy, the English teacher, and Dracula, who taught them science. The headmistress, Miss Flynn, was called Agatha Christie. They learned that she was called that because of her uncanny ability to find the guilty party when someone stepped out of line.

The first year classes were named after people in Irish History. David and Josie were in Davitt. They got to know the names of their classmates, and soon little groups formed of three or four who became special friends.

David was curious about one of his classmates, Fred Dardy, a boy not in his own group. The name was unusual; the only time David had seen it before was on the shop where the man had refused to sell him boots. One day he buttonholed the boy in the yard.

'Hi, Fred,' he said. 'I want to ask you something?'

'Yeah, go on.'

'Are you from the clothes shop in Morning Street?'

'Yeah. Sure everyone knows that.'

'I just wasn't sure,' David said.

'Why do you ask?'

'Nothing. It's just I tried to buy a pair of boots there one day and the man in the shop wouldn't sell them to me.'

Fred looked curiously at David.

'That was my dad,' he said. 'Did you not have the money or something?'

'No. It wasn't that. I – I don't know what it was really.'

David didn't want to drag Batt into it. He had an instinct that it was better not to dig up something that had lain buried for a long time. It wouldn't have been buried in the first place unless it ought to have been. He was sorry he had asked.

But he had awakened Fred Dardy's curiosity.

At the midday break the students floated in twos and threes around the town, in and out of shops and cafés – 'hanging around'. As the time to reassemble approached, they drifted back to the school yard, where some of them kicked a ball around the middle of the yard and others huddled in groups by the walls, chatting.

When David walked into the yard, he had an uneasy feeling of people looking at him and talking about him. Someone bleated like a sheep, 'Baa-baa-baa!' He turned around to see who it was but nobody was looking in his direction. Then someone behind his back bleated again.

Fred Dardy was at the centre of a group of five or six, all boys, talking to them, sniggering, and throwing a side eye at David. Fred said something, and the others turned in unison and stared at David, a sharp, curious look.

The bell rang and David moved towards his classroom. He found himself at the head of the queue because the others were hanging back to let him go ahead. Josie joined him.

'What's going on?' David asked her.

'What do you mean?'

'I don't know. I have a weird feeling that I'm in the news.'

'Are you sure?' Josie asked. 'You might be imagining it.'

Then a voice at the end of the line shouted, 'Killer's breed!' It was followed by the sheep-bleating again.

David kept looking straight ahead, but his heart beat faster and his mind went numb. 'Killer's breed' meant nothing to him, but he was certain that the words were shouted at himself.

Josie, however, turned and stared. She stood there and the line behind her stopped and waited. She searched the faces, trying to find out who had shouted. In the short time that they had been in the school Josie had become a kind of unofficial class leader. Nobody had appointed her, but all her classmates respected her.

'I think it was Ruction Moriarty,' she said when she turned around and walked on with David. 'He had an embarrassed look when I caught his eye.'

'Do you know what it's all about?' David asked.

'No, but can't we find out?'

'How?'

'We'll ask Ruction Moriarty.'

'What's the sheep noise about?' he asked.

'I know that's about Batt Andy.'

'What has that got to do with him?'

'Oh, you know,' Josie said, and she seemed reluctant to talk about it, 'about the way he looks after the sheep.'

David was puzzled. 'But everybody out in the glen looks after sheep. Why don't they get mocked?'

'Not like Batt Andy, they don't.'

'I don't get it,' David said. 'Why Batt and no one else?'

'It's the way he looks after them, talking to them and petting them like dogs and that.' Josie's voice faded as if she didn't want to embarrass him.

David was at a loss. 'What do you think I should do about it?' he asked.

'The same as Batt Andy does, nothing, and they'll get tired of it soon enough.'

David thought about it for a minute.

'I don't know if Ruction Moriarty's the one we should be talking to,' he said. 'I have an idea that Fred Dardy's behind it.'

'How do you know?'

'Just the way he looked when he was talking to a few of them in the yard.'

'OK then,' Josie said. 'Let's ask Fred.'

12

A Sad Time of Year

After school Josie and David went towards the bus. A small group stood near the gate, and someone among them shouted, 'Killer's breed!' Others bleated, 'Baa-baa-baa!' Josie walked boldly to the group and the leering smiles died on their faces. She spoke to Fred Dardy.

'Hi, Fred!' she said, singling him out as the one she wanted to talk to.

'What?' said Fred, trying to look as innocent as a baby.

'We want to talk.'

Fred looked right and left at his companions, a forced smile fixed on his lips, but his friends were silent and deadpan.

'OK, Josie,' Fred said, and he left the group and went with her to David.

'What's going on?' David asked him.

'Nothing!' Fred said, and he opened his eyes wide in a pretence of not knowing what they were talking about.

Neither Josie nor David spoke. They just stood and looked at him, waiting for an answer to the question. He shifted from foot to foot, and turned his head to look at his companions, but there was no encouragement from them, not even a supporting smile. He turned back and spoke to David.

'OK, OK,' he said. 'I'll tell you. It's about Batt Quilty.'

'What about him?' David asked.

Fred looked down at his toes. 'I don't like saying it,' he said.

'You didn't mind saying it to that clown, Ruction, who

shouted at Davy,' Josie said. 'You haven't got the bottle to say it to his face?'

'All right then,' Fred said crossly. 'Batt Quilty killed a man.'

David and Josie were struck speechless. The bus driver blew the horn, calling them aboard. They sat beside each other on the journey home, silent. When they got out at the glen, they let Eddie go ahead.

'Do you think he was telling the truth?' David asked.

'It must be something he heard.'

'I'm sure it's not true,' David said. 'But where did he get it? I must ask Batt.' He stopped. 'No, I can't. I just couldn't walk in and say "Did you kill a man?"'

'Don't say anything yet,' Josie said as he left her at her own gate. 'I'll ask my dad.'

David walked up the lane, his mind like a whirlpool. Batt just couldn't be a murderer. OK he was silent and didn't talk much, but there was no way he could be a murderer. That awful word!

But for a long time David had a suspicion that the quiet man carried some kind of dark secret. Mary Murdon had asked him if he minded going to Batt Andy's house; the house door was left open, but the tool-shed door was locked; Dardy had been so hostile in the clothes shop; the 'bit of bother that happened fifteen years before'. And now, Fred Dardy's poison!

In a strange way David wasn't too bothered to have something new to worry about. It took his mind from other things such as for example worrying about his dad.

✛ ✛ ✛

'What's the news?' Batt said as he carried the broad dish of potatoes to the table.

'Nothing out of the ordinary,' David said, and he nearly choked on the lie.

'Bringing them down tomorrow,' Batt said.

'Why? What's on?'

Batt was different when he talked about sheep. Whatever tied his tongue at other times was loosened then and his words ran free.

'A sad time of the year for me,' he said. 'Time for the cull.'

'The cull?'

'Parting with some of them tomorrow – lambs for the meat business, and the older ewes going to farms east in the good land.'

'What'll be left then?'

'The young ewes and the likely lambs. We'll be down to about four hundred animals – about all we can carry on our patch.'

David wondered what was so sad about it. 'But isn't that the way it's supposed to be?' he said.

'Yes, that's the way.'

'So what's sad?'

Batt didn't answer for a minute.

'I never say this,' Batt said, 'and I suppose it's a bit silly, but I hate to see them go. I go up the hill every day, and there they are, the same ones in the same places every day. They look up when I come into sight, and when they see it's me, they know that everything is all right, and they carry on grazing their own little piece of ground.'

'How do you know which is which?' David asked. 'They all look the same to me.'

'That's because you don't really look at them. If you did, you'd spot little differences, like the size and the shape of the head, the way the head is set on the neck, and other little things. It's like being able to tell people by their faces and so on.'

'I know people get very fond of dogs,' David said as he cleared the table and began to wash up at the sink. 'Dogs are always around people, and they're sort of clever, like Homer. Homer is one of the family, but I never thought people could feel the same about sheep or cows or that.'

'Sheep are the gentlest creatures of all,' Batt said. 'Have you any idea of what it's like up there on the top of that hill in the middle of winter?'

'No.'

'It's wet and windy, and at times there's frost, and, even when the snow melts down here, there's still a white blanket up there above the lake.'

'Do you bring them down in the snow?' David asked.

'No, I don't bring them down,' Batt said. 'They get over it well enough. But if the snow is thick and lying on the ground for a long time, I might bring them up hay or nuts.'

'On the tractor?'

'Good Lord! No. You couldn't bring a tractor up there. I bring the stuff up on my back. Look, when you're finished there, come out with me to check the fencing on the fold.'

David knew he could check the fencing on his own, but he was always trying to get the boy to take part.

'Will you manage on your own tomorrow?' David asked as they walked to the fold. He was hoping that Batt might ask him to give school a miss. He would be glad if he did. He didn't fancy being shouted at, especially being called 'Killer's breed'. He didn't know how to deal with that.

'No, I won't be on my own,' Batt answered his question. 'I'll have Homer, and he's worth ten men on a job like that.'

The fencing was sound, so they returned to the house.

'A letter there for you,' Batt said, pointing to an envelope leaning against a plate on the dresser. 'English postmark.'

It was a letter from David's dad.

Dear David,

Forgive me for leaving without getting in touch with you, and for not letting you have my address here. I felt I had to cut all ties with the old life and start afresh in a new place. 'Getting my act together,' you might call it. But know this: I have not abandoned you. When the time is right, I'll come for you.

It has become more urgent for me to do so since I've been told where you are and who you are with. Batt Quilty had no time for a person like me from an urban background, and he did all he could to keep your mother and me apart. Then a time came when he was accused of doing something that brought disgrace on his own family including us – no need for you to know the details. I wanted us to have nothing to do with him, but, naturally, your mother, may she rest in peace, would not agree to break her family ties in that kind of way. You'll be OK with him though until I can get you back home. At least it's better than going into care.

It has been tough for me here, a hard struggle to settle down and to fight my other problem, but I'm just about ready to come out the other end of the nightmare. So keep your heart up. It won't be long more now.

Lots of love from
Your Dad.

David folded the letter, placed it in the envelope, and put it between the pages of his history book in his school bag. He didn't speak, though his head was on fire. While he read the letter it was as if he could hear his father's voice, and it brought back to him his own home and the sadness that was part of it now. He thought he was coming through his bad time, but this letter put him back.

'Well?' Batt asked.

'Well, what?' David said gruffly.

'What has he got to say?'

'Nothing much. He's OK and he'll be coming home soon. I want to go for a walk!'

David went out, crossed over the rampart and strode along the valley towards the Germans' farm. He should be glad that his father was well and would be home soon. And he was. There was no doubt about that. But he wasn't as happy about it as he should be, and he knew it was because the letter opened up old wounds.

13

Battle Frenzy

'Go on, tell me!' David said when he sat beside Josie in the bus next morning.

'I would if I knew.'

'Sorry,' David said. 'I thought you were going to find out.'

'My dad said Batt didn't kill Tim the Fiddler, but that was all. He said it was a long story.'

'Tim the Fiddler?'

'Yes.'

'But what happened? Was someone arrested for it? Why was Batt's name mixed up in it?'

'I don't know. Dad just shut up when I asked him.'

David was disappointed. All he had found out was that Tim the Fiddler had been killed, and that some people believed Batt had something to do with it. Fred Dardy for one. No, not Fred. His father!

The shouters behind corners and the whisperers in the classroom changed their taunt from 'Killer's breed' to just 'Killer'. Several times during the day David heard them, always someone behind his back and in a crowd. He couldn't pick out the shouter or the whisperer, or the sheep impersonators. He began to feel tense and nervous.

When the students got back to the school after the lunch break, they swarmed to the locker room to get their textbooks for the afternoon classes. David took his science book and his history book, locked the door of his locker and turned to walk to the classroom. His way was blocked by five or six boys, mainly from more senior classes. Standing in the centre was Fred Dardy, his mouth spread in a silly grin.

One of the group spoke, 'Hey mane, what's that book you have there?'

It was Barry Moriarty, the boy known as 'Ruction'. He was a pale, strong-limbed boy, about a year older than David. His blonde hair was cut short and covered his head like the stubble on an autumn cornfield. He was a wild one. Wherever there was a dust-up or a hullabaloo Ruction was sure to be at the centre of it. The quieter ones gave him a lot of space.

He seemed to enjoy his fierce reputation, and had developed a tough way of speaking, a slow drawl. He began most sentences with 'Hey man' though it came out more like 'Hey mane'.

David let him take the science book out of his hand. He held it up and made a show of reading the title. '*Murder in Glenfune*, by Bartholomew Quilty,' he said. He held the book up for all to see, and said, 'Hey mane, you shouldn't be reading stuff like that. It might be, like, bad for you.'

His hangers-on laughed.

'Well, at least I can read,' David said. 'It looks like you have a problem.'

The laughing stopped.

'Hey mane, take that back!' Ruction said.

'I can't. It's true,' David said.

'I said, take it back.'

'No! If you can't read what's on the cover of that book, then you have a real problem.'

'You're dead, mane!' and Ruction raised a fist.

David had no violent hatred of Ruction. But, with his fierce anger at the way he was being picked on by his schoolmates, he was like a can of hot petrol ready to explode at the touch of a tiny spark.

Ruction was not expecting the blow to his nose. He probably thought that this newcomer would give way to him as all the others did. He staggered back against the wall, then stood there, his eyes popping in surprise, and two trickles of blood began to flow from his nostrils.

David took the book from Ruction's flabbergasted hand and tucked it under his arm with the others. Then he turned away and began to move in the direction of his classroom. He was alert, however, to a probable retaliation, and it came. When Ruction swung his fist, David ducked, and the blow intended for him landed with a resounding crash on the door of a nearby locker.

The fight was on. They punched each other from one end of the locker room to the other. Ruction was stronger, but David had that build-up of volcanic fury caged like a wild beast within him, and now he set it free. It didn't matter how many times Ruction hit him, he kept advancing, his own arms flailing and his fists landing somewhere on Ruction.

The fight lasted only a few minutes in all. Boys gathered from every corner of the locker room to watch. They stood around, cheering, not taking sides, just exulting in the tumult of battle.

As many toughies do, Ruction began to wilt in the face of David's persistence. He stopped punching and crossed his arms before his face to ward off David's attack.

Then someone shouted, 'Dracula!' At once the onlookers fell silent and scattered to their own lockers as if nothing had happened. But the combatants carried on, too engrossed to realise that authority, in the person of Dracula, the science teacher, was present.

Dracula caught the two fighters by the collars of their shirts and dragged them apart. They stood facing each other, panting.

71

David was still raging, but Ruction apparently had had enough. His eyes were downcast and he sagged in the grip of Dracula.

'What's all this about?' Dracula asked.

Neither of the warriors spoke.

'Well, if you don't want to tell me, that's all right. Go to Miss Flynn's office and tell her what it's all about.'

'Only a bit of fun, sir,' Ruction said.

'It didn't look very funny to me,' Dracula replied. 'Go ahead to Miss Flynn's office. Maybe she'll see the joke. She is renowned for her sense of humour.'

They went to the headmistress's office. As they made their way slowly down the corridor, Ruction said, 'We'll tell her we were only playing.'

David didn't answer.

'Only playing, OK?' Ruction said again.

'I wasn't playing,' David said.

'Come in,' Miss Flynn called in answer to Ruction's knock.

They went in and stood before her desk. She was writing something.

'Well?' she said, still with her head down.

'Mr Dennehy sent us,' Ruction said.

Miss Flynn put down the pen and looked from one to the other.

'Well?' she said again. 'Are you going to keep it a secret?'

'We were playing, Miss.' Ruction was the spokesman.

'Oh! And what form did your game take?'

'Boxing, Miss. We were playing boxing.'

'I see. Judging by the blood on your nose and the swelling under your eye, your play was in virtual reality mode. Would I be right?'

'Yes, Miss.'

She paused and looked at David.

'Have you anything to say for yourself, Mr – Mr – what is your name?'

'David Lakes, Miss.'

'Ah, yes. The boy from Glenfune. Well, have you anything to say.'

'We were fighting, Miss.'

'Why?'

David hung his head and didn't speak.

'I see,' she said, and she turned to Ruction.

'Well, Mr Moriarty, would you like to tell me what you were fighting about.'

'It – it wasn't my fault, Miss.'

'Good! Now, enlighten me. What wasn't your fault?'

'He said I couldn't read, Miss.'

She turned to David. 'What couldn't he read?'

'The name of my science book, Miss.'

She asked him for the book, handed it to Ruction and asked him to read the title. He read it.

'So, why did David accuse you of not being able to read it?'

Gradually, by dint of question after question, she got the whole story from them. By then Ruction was in a panic. It was as if he hadn't realised the wickedness of what he had been saying until the moment that Miss Flynn held him in her clear-eyed, steady gaze and said, 'So you thought it would be fun to ridicule David by calling his grandfather a murderer?'

'No, Miss,' Ruction spluttered. 'You see, Miss, I didn't know anything about it. It wasn't me at all, really, Miss.'

'Not you? 'I see. Very well, then, Barry. Would you mind telling me, if it wasn't you, who was it?'

'Fred Dardy, Miss.'

'Go on. Tell me exactly what Fred Dardy had to do with it.'

Ruction looked at David and hung his head. He didn't speak.

Miss Flynn turned to David.

'You can go back to your class, David.'

David turned and as he was opening the door, Miss Flynn said, 'Ask Fred Dardy to come to my office, please; and I may want to speak to you again.'

14

The Box of Secrets

Next morning David studied the faces in the yard, searching for Fred or Ruction. He wanted to find out what Agatha Christie had said to them. But they were missing.

'Maybe she suspended them,' Josie said.

'She would hardly do that just for calling me names,' David said.

'That depends on the names.'

Later that morning, when they were in class, David spotted Fred Dardy and his father hurrying past the classroom window. They were on their way to the main door and the Head's office. Half an hour went by and they passed the window again on the way out.

Later again Ruction and his mother went in. After about ten minutes Mrs Moriarty left by herself. Ruction must have gone to his classroom.

When school was over, David and Josie strolled toward the bus. Ruction was there, standing to the side of the queue as if counting the students on their way into the bus. They noticed that he had a black eye.

'What does he want?' Josie asked, anxious.

'Don't worry about him,' David said. 'He's harmless. He's not so bad really.'

'Hey, Lakes,' Ruction called when he saw them.

They stopped and waited for him to speak.

'Can I talk to you for a minute?' he said, looking at David.

David stepped out of the queue and Josie went with him.

'About yesterday,' Ruction said.

David didn't say anything.

'Well, OK,' Josie said. 'What about yesterday?'

'Hey, mane, I'm really sorry,' Ruction said, and he sounded sincere. 'I didn't wise up on the real scene. I figured it for a bit of slagging. How was I to know it was for real?'

'Who said that it was for real?' Josie asked.

'Agatha Christie. She wised up my ma. Dardy wouldn't say sorry because his old man wouldn't give in; stuck to his guns, said it was gospel.'

'What did she say to you?'

'She said I couldn't come back until I apologised.'

'Is that why you apologised?' Josie asked.

'Yeah. My mother too. She put the squeeze on me.' He frowned and waved his hand in a gesture dismissing what he had said. 'No. No! That's not why I'm sorry. 'Twas just I didn't cop 'twas real. I figured it only for slagging.'

David remained silent.

'Are we OK so?' Ruction persisted.

'Yeah, it's OK,' David said.

'Cool, mane! See you!'

Ruction took off and ran away towards the street.

✛   ✛   ✛

'What are you thinking?' David asked as the bus moved out of the town.

'I'm just wondering why it was such a big deal for Fred to say he was sorry. Why couldn't he just pretend – if 'twas only to get Agatha Christie off his back?'

They left the bus at the mouth of the glen, and walked along the road through the glen, past Murdons' house, past Tim the Fiddler's. They looked at the ruined cottage.

'I don't even know how it happened.' David said. 'Was he shot or stabbed or what?'

'Don't bother your head about it,' Josie said. 'It's all over now. They won't be calling you those names again.'

'How do you know that?'

'I know. Word will get out. They'll know that Fred Dardy is suspended, and Ruction will tell everyone why. Ruction himself certainly won't do it.'

'We'll see,' David said.

When he topped the rampart, he saw Batt chopping wood on the block. The block was a thick round of a tree trunk, which they used as a chopping block. David looked at his grandfather swinging the axe, and he wondered how Ned Farren was so sure that Batt hadn't done it. David himself knew he hadn't. He had no proof, but he just knew.

'Your dinner is on the range,' Batt said as David arrived. 'Help yourself. I have to go into town. I might not get back until after dark. Do the few jobs.'

✛ ✛ ✛

Batt went away in the old Ford. David stood at the door listening to the sound of it dying away until it was gone out of earshot at the mouth of the glen.

He ate his dinner and washed up, then fed Homer and tied the goats to the iron peg at the back of the house. It was still daylight, though the sun had gone over the hills to the west. The dark was gathering in the corners of the kitchen, so he switched on the light to do his homework. At least he intended to do his homework, but he wasn't able to concentrate.

He closed his maths book and went outside. He ambled to the top of the rampart and watched the glen, quiet and fading into the deepening dark. A light showed in Farrens' window. That was the living-room, and he imagined the 'young ones' seated around the table at homework. Further on towards the mouth of the glen a light winked too in Murdons' window. Nearer to him was the ruin of Tim the Fiddler's old house, without light and full of mystery.

If that ruin could tell its secrets, what would it say? Nothing! If he were to find out anything about the murder, it would have to come from some other place.

'The box!'

He remembered the box under Batt's bed. He had heard him moving it the day he put the letter about himself away. 'After dark,' he had said. He would be home after dark. There was very little time.

David ran into the house and up to Batt's bedroom. It was a simple room, with only the bare necessities of a bedroom – a bed, a wardrobe, a bedside locker with an alarm clock that ticked loudly in the quiet house. The window was closed, shutting out the cool evening air.

David got down on his knees and looked under the bed. It was there, an old-fashioned wooden trunk. It was heavy and he had to use all his strength to pull it out. There was no lock, so he opened it. It contained bundles of papers tied with string, and a black, tin cash box with a lock. There was also a biscuit tin full to the top with letters. They were addressed to Batt. David recognised the handwriting. They were letters from his mother.

He opened one. It began, *Dear Dad*. It was eerie. Her voice sounded in his head and he couldn't bear the sadness that hit him like a blow. He put the letter back in its envelope and put it back in the biscuit tin. He examined some of the papers. They were receipts, bills, Department of Agriculture leaflets, and circulars from suppliers.

At the bottom of the pile he found a plain school exercise book, a sum copy, lined with squares. *Interviews with the gardaí* was written on the cover in that old-fashioned, stylish writing that old people had. Batt's name in full and his address were written there: *Bartholomew J. Quilty, Knocklee, Glenfune, Coombowler, Co. Kerry.* David opened it and began to read. It was written in a kind of legal language, as if Batt were giving evidence in court.

This is what David read:

The following is an account of an interview with the guards in Coombowler garda station which took place yesterday, the 27th of May in the year 1980, given by me, Bartholomew John Quilty. It is written on the day following the interview and is accurate to the best of my memory.

Detective Garda Sergeant Mooney offered me a cup of tea, which I declined, and he said that I was entitled to have my solicitor present while I was being questioned.

Quilty: I am as innocent as a newborn child and don't need anyone present.

Mooney: All the same I think you should have your solicitor here.

Quilty: This is beginning to sound nasty. I have nothing to hide from you, and I haven't done anything that would need a solicitor to be here while I'm answering you.'

Mooney: Who is your solicitor?

Quilty: John Falvey, but I don't need him here.

Mooney: If you like, we could give him a ring. I think it mightn't be any harm if he were with you.

Quilty: Well, if it would make you happy, go ahead and ring him. I couldn't care less.

Just then David heard the sound of the Ford changing gear as it turned into the lane and began the climb up the hill toward the house. He put the copy back and pushed the trunk under the bed. When Batt came in, he was seated at the table, working on a problem in quadratic equations.

15

Interrogation

'Are you coming up the hill?' Batt asked after the dinner on Saturday.

'Can I cry off today?' David asked. 'We've an essay for Monday and I don't want to leave it until tomorrow if I can.'

'OK, so. I won't be too long.' Batt said, and he was gone.

David watched through the window as man and dog made their way up the hill. When they were near the top, approaching the lake, he reckoned he would have time enough to study the sum copy. Batt couldn't be back for well over an hour.

David brought the copy down to the kitchen and sat at the table to read it. From there he could still keep an eye out for Batt returning. He read from where he had stopped the day before, when Batt's solicitor, John Falvey had been sent for.

[Mr John Falvey arrived after about ten minutes. He had a consultation with me in private and assured me that I had nothing to worry about. He advised me to be truthful in my answers to the questions of the gardaí. The interview was conducted by Detective Garda Sergeant Mooney and Detective Garda Spain. It was recorded on tape.

A uniformed garda brought in a slashhook wrapped in a plastic bag and laid it on the table.]

Mooney: Have a look at that. Can you tell us what it is?
[I examined it.]
Quilty: It's a slasher. It's mine. Did you take it out of the shed?

Mooney: No. It was found a short distance from the victim's house. Do you see those brown stains on the blade?

Quilty: I do.

Mooney: That's blood. It will be examined and if the blood type matches that of the dead man, we can be fairly sure it's the murder weapon. Can you give us any idea why it turned up so close to the victim's house?

Quilty: Somebody must have taken it out of my shed. That's all.

Mooney: When did you see it last?

Quilty: Must be three or four months ago when I was clearing furze at the side of the meadow. Did you get fingerprints off it? Wouldn't that tell you who had it?

Mooney: There were no fingerprints on it. Could you give us an account of your movements on the 19th, last Monday?

Quilty: The day before I found Tim?

Mooney: Yes.

Quilty: That day, after dinner, I saw Pete Murdon coming down the hill, and he came to me with the news that some of my flock was gone down the north side of the hill, after breaking through the fence. I took the stick and called the dog and up we went. Someone was after cutting the fence and the sheep were gone. By the time we had driven them back and the fence mended, it was nearly dark. I was lucky to make it home before the pitch black dark had set in.

Then, in the evening, I went down to Tim the Fiddler's to finish off a deal I was doing with him the evening before to buy his farm. We made the deal for fourteen thousand for the land, but not the house, and we shook hands on it. I was to pick him up next morning to bring him into town to sign the papers.

Mooney: And you didn't go out after that?

Quilty: No. I was inside for the night.

Mooney: You said that someone had cut the fence. How do you know that?

Quilty: Because I have two eyes in my head. Didn't I see it cut, a clean *cut, in every strand from the ground up? You can go up and see it for your-self.*

Mooney: You said you mended it.

Quilty: I did. I drew the strands together and twisted them around each other.

Mooney: Will that hold?

Quilty: It will of course. The sheep aren't going to unravel them. Any-way the break was at the other side of the gully, and the sheep would never go there, unless someone drove them.

Mooney: You're sure of that?

Quilty: Of course I'm sure.

Mooney: And you can't explain the slashhook being where we found it?

Quilty: It's easy enough to explain it. Someone must have put it there. And if you say it was the murder weapon with blood on it, they must have put it there after doing for poor old Tim.

Mooney: So you're saying that a mysterious 'someone' cut your fence, drove your sheep through the gap, and, while you were chasing them, took your slashhook and killed Tim Heffernan with it?

Quilty: I'm not saying that. You are. I'm just telling you what happened to me last Monday.

Mooney: Thank you, Mr Quilty. That will be all for now.

An account of a second interview began on a new page.

The following is an account of an interview with the guards in Coom-bowler garda station which took place yesterday, the 29th of May in the year 1980. This interview was conducted by Detective Inspector Carey from Cork City, and he was accompanied by Detective Garda Sergeant Mooney.

Carey: You have already told us that you were trying to buy the Heffer-nan land, but we have reason to believe that old Tim had refused to sell. We also have reason to believe that you were telling lies when you said that Pete Murdon had told you that some of your sheep had strayed down the other side of the hill.

Quilty: Now why would you think that was a lie?

Carey: Pete Murdon doesn't remember ever having that conversation with you. What have you to say about that?

Quilty: Poor old Pete's memory is not very reliable.

Carey: Why do you say that?

Quilty: Because that's the sort he is. He isn't known for having a memory, good or bad. Have you checked the break in the fence up there on the hill?

Mooney: It's there all right, but it could have been done months ago. There's no way of knowing that it was done last week or the week before or whenever it was done.

Quilty: You think I did it for fun?

Carey: No. But you might have done it to cover your tracks. You say you went over the hill to round up some stray sheep on the day of the murder. Did anyone see you?

Quilty: Maybe.

Carey: Who?

Quilty: I don't know. People are always looking around on the hill, curious about what everyone else is doing. We haven't much else to be doing in Glenfune.

Carey: How did your slashhook get down to Tim Heffernan's place? Incidentally, we have established that the bloodstains on the blade match his blood type.

Quilty: I answered that already. I don't know. Did you find any fingerprints on the handle of the slasher?

Carey: No.

Quilty: Isn't that strange?

Carey: Not necessarily.

Quilty: Look, if you have no more questions for me, I want to be getting back home. You have embarrassed me a lot already. People are avoiding me and looking at me in a strange way. I think they have already convicted me.

Carey: We may want to talk to you again, Mr Quilty. We'll drop you back home for now.

16

Snow on High Ground

In December it snowed all one night and the ground was covered in the morning. David joined the Farrens and they planted fresh footprints on the snow on their way to the mouth of the glen. The school bus didn't turn up, so they had to go home again and David was able to go with Batt to feed the sheep.

First they pulled out some hay and tied it with rope so that David could sling it over his shoulder. Batt took his own bundle, about twice as big as David's, and they set out for the hill. On the first part of the climb the snow lay thinly on the ground. Then, above the lake, their feet were plunging into about six inches of it, and near the top it was almost a foot deep.

At one point there was a deep drift of snow and Batt threw down his bundle of hay and scraped the snow aside with his hands, burrowing through the drift, until he came upon a sheep standing still at the bottom.

'They always turn their backs to the falling snow,' he explained to David. 'Then they just stand there and let it gather on top of them.'

He took the sheep's head between his hands and spoke gently to it, 'You poor innocent thing,' he said. 'You'd freeze under the snow rather than run away from it.'

He went to the bundle, pulled some hay from it and threw it to the sheep.

They found two other sheep buried and they cleared the

snow away from them. Then they walked along the hill, leaving some hay here and there.

'They haven't enough sense to dig down to the grass,' Batt said. 'The poor things are so helpless.'

'But other animals would have a problem with that too,' David said.

'No. The reindeer in Lapland and places like that dig with their hooves down to the grazing.'

✢ ✢ ✢

They had come down the steepest part of the hill, and were walking easily down the lower slope.

'I'd like to talk to you about something,' David began.

'About Tim the Fiddler, I suppose.'

David stood, and Batt stood, not looking at him but across the hill towards Tim the Fiddler's house. He waited for David to speak.

'How did you know what I was going to talk about?' David asked.

'I knew you were mooching around in my box upstairs, and I guessed that you were at the copy book.'

'How did you know?'

'You must have put them away in a hurry that first day,' Batt said, and he laughed. 'The copy was at the bottom. I always keep it over the newspaper cuttings. In proper order, don't you understand.'

'No, I don't.' David thought for a while. 'But what made you look at it? Don't tell me you look at it every day. It's been there for about fifteen years now.'

'No,' Batt said. 'You made one big mistake that put me on to you.'

'What was that?'

'You closed the door of my bedroom. I always let it open,

87

especially in cold weather. I close all the windows and open all the doors inside the house to let the heat of the fire circulate through all the rooms.'

'Batt Quilty's central heating system,' David mocked.

'I'm always saying, you'll meet yourself coming back. What was it you wanted to say about Tim the Fiddler.'

'Just one thing I'd like to know,' David said. 'Did the guards charge you? What happened?'

'A good question,' Batt said. 'If you had kept your wits about you when you were snooping in my box, you wouldn't have to ask it.'

'What do you mean?'

'Because I had all the newspaper reports of my trial at the bottom of the box. The answer to your question was there for you to see.'

'I didn't know what the newspaper cuttings were about.'

'You didn't look too hard. No matter. When we get back, I'll let you have a read of them.'

'Just tell me one other thing,' David said, 'Why did you write down the account of your interviews with the guards?'

'I thought they might charge me and I wanted to set it down while it was fresh in my mind in case my lawyers might want to know.'

17

The Trial

When they got back to the house, Batt went upstairs, and David heard him moving the box. He came down, bringing the newspaper cuttings, and handed them to David.

All of the cuttings had a date pencilled in and the name of the paper.

Coombowler Observer Wednesday 21st May 1980. The heading said Man Found Dead. David read on:

A man, believed to be in his seventies, was found dead yesterday morning in his house in Glenfune near the village of Tubber. The victim has been identified as Timothy Heffernan, known locally as Tim the Fiddler. The gardaí are treating his death as suspicious.

The second cutting was dated Friday 6th June 1980.
Man arrested for Glenfune Murder
Gardaí yesterday arrested and charged Bartholomew Quilty of Knocklee, Glenfune, Coombowler, with the murder of his neighbour Timothy Heffernan at the victim's home in Glenfune last month. People in the locality were shocked to hear of the developments.

'We're all dazed,' a neighbour said to our reporter. 'Nothing like that ever happened in this place before.'

The third cutting: Wednesday 7th October 1980
Murder Trial Opens
The trial began in the High Court, Dublin, yesterday of Bartholomew

Quilty of Glenfune, Coombowler, Co. Kerry, for the murder, on 20th of May, of Timothy Heffernan.

Mr Fitzhenry, for the prosecution, outlined the circumstances of the murder for the jury of eight men and four women. Mr Heffernan's body was found by the defendant and the gardaí were informed by him on the morning of 20th May.

'The murder was a particularly vicious and brutal act,' Mr Fitzhenry said. 'The victim was struck a savage blow with a sharp, heavy instrument on the back of the neck and died shortly afterwards.

Evidence of identification of the body was given by Mary Murdon, a neighbour. Mr Heffernan had no known relatives alive.

The court was adjourned until ten o'clock this morning. The trial is expected to last three days.

The fourth cutting: Thursday 9th October 1980
Suspect ' ... had a funny look!'

On the second day of the trial of Bartholomew Quilty of Glenfune, Coombowler, Co. Kerry, for the murder, on 20th of May, of Timothy Heffernan evidence was given by Detective Inspector Carey of arresting the accused and charging him. The accused replied, 'That's all wrong. I had nothing to do with it.'

Mr Pete Murdon of Glenfune told Mr Walter Fitzhenry, for the prosecution, that he saw Batt Quilty coming out of Heffernan's house at about 9 p.m. on the evening of the murder. He had a 'funny' look about him, and he hurried away towards his own house.

Cross-examined by Mr Lawrence Roche, for the defendant, Mr Murdon answered 'No' to every question put to him. He denied that he had ever seen the slashhook produced. He denied that either he or his sister had gone to see Mr Heffernan after the defendant had left on that evening. He had not spoken to Batt Quilty on the 20th of May. He had not told Batt Quilty that his sheep had strayed on to Cronin's land at the top of Knocklee.

'Can you say anything but "No"?' Mr Roche asked.

'No!'

(Laughter)

Mr Murdon's sister, Mary, admitted that she frequently visited Tim Heffernan while he was alive, that she brought him his dinner every day. She did it just to be neighbourly. She denied that she was trying to get into his good graces in the hope of being left his farm in his will. She also denied that she had tutored her brother, Pete, on his evidence in court.

The trial was adjourned until today.

The fifth cutting: Friday 10th October 1980
Accused Acquitted

The murder trial of Bartholomew Quilty of Glenfune, Coombowler, Co. Kerry, for the murder, on 20th of May, of Timothy Heffernan, came to an abrupt end yesterday in the High Court. The defendant, questioned by Mr Laurence Roche for the defence, said that on the afternoon of Tuesday 19th of May he had been alerted by a neighbour, Mr Pete Murdon, to a breakout of some of his sheep at the top of Knocklee. He went to the place and found that the fence wire had been cut and about fifty of his flock had gone and were grazing on the land of Michael Cronin. He drove them back and repaired the fence.

That evening he went to see the victim, in order to complete a deal involving the purchase of Mr Heffernan's farm.

He made the deal to buy the farm, and he agreed to bring Mr Heffernan to the solicitor's office in Coombowler on the following morning in order to complete the paper work. When he called at 9 a.m. on the following morning he found Mr Heffernan lying dead in his bedroom. He went to Tubber and phoned the gardaí.

Cross-examined by Mr Fitzhenry, he identified as his the slashhook produced.

Mr Fitzhenry: How do you account for it turning up in the back garden of Tim Heffernan's house the day after the murder?

Mr Quilty: Somebody must have taken it out of my shed. That's all.

Mr Fitzhenry: When did you see it last?

Mr Quilty: Must be three or four months before that when I was clearing furze at the side of the meadow.

Mr Fitzhenry: Are you absolutely sure of that?

Mr Quilty: Will you have sense, man! If I wanted to kill poor old Tim, would I do it with my own slasher and leave it thrown in his garden for any gom to find after me?

Mr Justice Connolly intervened at that stage, and directed the jury to find the defendant not guilty because of insufficient evidence to secure a conviction. Mr Quilty was released.

18

Suspicions

'It was Pete Murdon did it!' David said excitedly.

'Why do you say that?' Batt asked.

'Isn't it obvious. Either you or Pete was lying. You weren't, so he must have been.'

'How do you know I wasn't lying?'

'I just know.'

'All right. Even if Pete was lying, that's not to say that he did it.'

'But why else would he be telling lies about it?' David asked.

'He could be telling lies for any number of reasons,' Batt said. 'Anyway, poor Pete isn't always too sure about what's real and what's fancy. If he hadn't Mary to look after him, he'd be in a right pucker.'

'Well the guards should have questioned him about it.'

'Maybe they did. The guards had a choice of chasing him or me. They picked on me, I suppose because of the slasher.'

'But that wasn't fair.'

'Fair doesn't come into it. Look, Davy, put it out of your mind. It happened a long time ago and let it there.'

'But some people still think that you did it, and that's not right.'

'Very few people think it now, or then either, and I'm not bothered about the ones who do.'

Batt closed the copybook and took it upstairs without another word.

✛ ✛ ✛

David was surprised one day when Ruction Moriarty invited him to his home at lunchtime.

'My mother said to ask you,' Ruction told him.

'Why?'

'Don't know, mane. She just said she'd like to have, like, a chat. I was to bring you home at lunchtime some day.'

'OK,' David said. 'I'll go tomorrow.'

Mrs Sarah Moriarty was a tall, blonde woman with a ready smile.

'So you're Davy Lakes,' she said. 'You're welcome here.'

'Thanks, Mrs Moriarty.'

'I'm glad you and Barry can be friends,' she said. 'That was an awful thing he shouted at you. He deserved the black eye you gave him.'

David was embarrassed. 'I'm sorry I lost my temper,' he said.

Ruction's father, Sorley, came in, a large, square man in a garda uniform. David hadn't known that he was a garda.

'Good man,' he said when Ruction introduced David. 'You taught this fellow a lesson. He thought he was the heavyweight champ of Coombowler Community College until you came along.'

David didn't know what to say. The Moriartys made light of his fight with Ruction as if it had been a sporting contest, but to him it was an outburst of bad temper, and he wanted to forget about it.

They sat down to lunch. Ruction's younger brother, Donagh, was there too.

'You must find it lonely out there in Glenfune,' Ruction's dad said.

'No. Not really,' David said. 'It's a great place, and there's always something to do on the farm.'

'I know Glenfune well,' Garda Moriarty said, and he took a sip of his tea. 'A good many years ago now I had the job of going out there once a year doing the farm census. I travelled over every inch of that glen road on a bike more times than I like to remember.'

David said nothing. 'I wonder was he there fifteen years ago?' he thought. He started to ask the question, 'So —,' he began, then stopped. It wasn't a question to be asked while all the others were sitting there.

'What is it?' Garda Moriarty asked.

'Nothing!'

'More bread, please!' Donagh butted in, and the moment passed.

'Call in any time,' Ruction's mother said when they were going back to school, and she turned to Ruction, 'Bring him again, Barry.'

'My dad is wise to something about that killing out there,' Ruction said as they walked together up the main street.

'Did he tell you?'

'No, but when he heard what had happened in school, he said what we'd shouted at you was a goddamn lie. He chewed me off about it.'

'Did he say any more?'

'No, and when I tried to get a bit more out of him, he told me to get lost.'

'Do you think he might tell me if I asked him?'

'Naw. He never talks about police stuff. Ma is forever giving him a hard time about that, having to get things off the paper, even when they're about himself.'

✢ ✢ ✢

A few days later David got a chance to talk to Ruction's father. He didn't have to do anything. It just happened. At lunchtime he had to go to Geaney's hardware shop for staples for Batt. As he strolled down the wide main street, a car pulled into the kerb beside him. It was a garda car and Sorley Moriarty was its driver and only occupant. He called David.

'Hop in there,' he said. 'I want to talk to you.'

'Well?' Garda Moriarty said when David was sitting in the passenger seat.

'What?' said David.

'You were going to ask me something the other day at lunchtime, but you stopped.'

'I know.'

'A wise move. No point in discussing private business with half the country listening. I'm sure you wanted to ask me something about the Tim the Fiddler business. It must be bothering you a lot.'

'Were you here at that time?' David asked.

'I was and for a few years before it.'

David was silent. He didn't know what question to ask.

'Your grandfather didn't do it,' Sorley Moriarty said quietly. 'I'd like you to know that in case it might be troubling you.'

'If he didn't do it, why did you people arrest him and bring him to court?' David asked petulantly.

'Because a detective from Cork was put in charge of the case, and he was going on a few bits of useless evidence that turned up. I told them they had it wrong when they charged him, but they wouldn't listen to me. I knew the people out that way, and I knew Batt Quilty would never do a thing like that.'

'But how can you be sure?' David asked. 'I know he didn't do it, but the court let him go only because they hadn't enough evidence.'

The garda gazed out the window for a long time. 'All I'm going to say is that the detective would have been better off looking hard at the ones living in Dardy's farms.'

'What farms?'

'Dardy's.'

'Where are Dardy's farms?'

'They're in a ring around this town and two of them are in Glenfune. No. Only one now in Glenfune.'

'That's not right. There are only four farms in Glenfune, ours, Farrens', Murdons' and the Germans'. Five farms when Tim the Fiddler was alive.'

'Murdons' farm is Dardy's,' the garda said. 'Mary Murdon rents it from him. The Germans' farm was his too, but he sold it to them.'

'But … but …,' David was dumbfounded. 'Murdons got their place from their father. Batt told me.'

'He didn't tell you any lie. Murdons did own it, but now it's Dardy's. He came by it around twenty years ago.

'How do you know all that?' David asked.

'Wasn't I the one who did the farm census?'

'But owning all those farms doesn't say that Dardy had anything to do with Tim the Fiddler. There's no crime in owning farms, is there?'

'No. But it might be interesting to know how he came by them.'

'If it was wrong, why wasn't he arrested?'

'You can't arrest people on suspicion, and that's all it was, only suspicion. You couldn't get anything out of your crowd out there in Glenfune. You won't be talking about it, will you?'

'There's nothing to be talking about.'

'Right! Off you go now and remember what I said. You have nothing to be worried about.'

David was a few minutes late getting back to school. He had dawdled along, the things Garda Moriarty said to him barging around inside his head. He guessed that the garda told him those things to make up for Ruction shouting 'Killer' at him. Ruction's parents seemed to be very put out about that.

19

Batt with a Halo

The time to the Christmas holidays rolled slowly by, and one day the postman delivered two Christmas cards for David – one from Susan Branagan, and the other one from her mother and father.

Susan's card was accompanied by a letter.

Dear David,

A happy Christmas. We haven't heard from you for a long time, and we are all wondering how you are getting on in the wilderness.

Things are very exciting here. Our first term is nearly down in Xantia Academy for Girls and we are rehearsing for the Christmas concert. I'm in the choir and I'm doing a solo turn as part of the programme, reciting Patrick Kavanagh's poem, 'A Christmas Childhood'.

We are having a junior disco on Thursday the 21st. That's the night before we get the holidays. The boys from St Andrew's will be there too. It is being held in our school hall. A pity you are so far away. Are you having anything like that in your school?

Mam and Dad said to tell you to write and let us know how you are.

Your friend,
Susan.

David was excited when he got the cards and letter, not just because of getting them but because of an idea it put in his head. He could talk to Mr Branagan about Tim the Fiddler, and, maybe, find out what he should do about it.

He got a Christmas card in town the next day and wrote to Susan.

Dear Sue,

Thanks for your letter and card. They came yesterday. I hope mine gets to you in time for Christmas. I hope you and all the family have a good time.

I'm getting on fine at school. We don't have concerts and stuff like discos for Christmas, but we will next term. Some of the teachers I like and some I don't. I like Dracula, the science and maths teacher, and Starchy, the English teacher. The others are all right, but I don't like Thorny the geography teacher. The head is Agatha Christie. She's sound.

I was wondering if you would like to come down some time for a visit. Batt, my grandad, isn't much for inviting, but I think he wouldn't mind if you came.

Say hello to your mam and dad for me.

Your friend David.

PS. Let me know if you decide to come down for a visit.

✛ ✛ ✛

He decided to tell Josie about his talk with Garda Moriarty. It was true that Garda Moriarty told him to keep it to himself, but he hadn't agreed to that. And, anyway, Josie wasn't just anyone. She had been in it with him from the beginning. She wouldn't breathe a word of it to anyone.

She wasn't surprised when he told her about Dardy's farms.

'I remember when I was young Mom going into town once a month and into Dardy's shop, handing in money and old Dardy writing in a passbook she brought with her. She told me she was paying for clothes she got for us.'

'Just clothes?' David asked.

'Yes. Well, that was it in the beginning. I remember when we came home, Dad always asked the same question, "Did you give it to him?" and Mom just said, "I did."'

'Must have been a big deal,' David said.

Josie gave him her mother's account of what happened.

It was in bad times, a number of years before Josie was born, and the Farrens found it hard to make ends meet. Ewart Dardy let them have clothes on tick, and not only that, but he offered to lend them money to tide them over. Ned wouldn't take a loan from him at first, but later on he had no choice.

The Farrens knew very little about loans and money business, so when Dardy mentioned interest on their loan, they agreed, not knowing exactly what it meant. Three pence per pound per month didn't sound too much to them, and, at first, when they hadn't borrowed a whole lot, they had no trouble in making the monthly payments.

But, as time went by, they had to borrow more and more, and a day came when they couldn't pay even the monthly interest. Ned was desperate and one day he told Batt Quilty about his troubles.

Josie stopped at that point and looked up towards the rampart and the puff of smoke rising from the house beyond. There was a catch in her voice as she said: 'Batt Andy gave him the money to pay off his debt.'

She stopped again and looked up at the rampart. 'Mom says that Batt is a saint,' she said.

David had a sudden image of Batt floating around in the

clouds with a halo around his cap. He couldn't imagine him taking that cap off even to be a saint. He laughed.

'What are you laughing at?' Josie asked, clearly offended that he should laugh at her show of feeling.

'Nothing,' he said. 'I was laughing at the idea of Batt wearing a halo. Sorry, it just jumped into my head when you said he was a saint.'

'It's not a joke,' Josie said, and there were tears in her voice. 'Just think of what it meant to us. We could have lost our farm and our home.'

'Oh, God! I know that,' David said, trying to make up for his callous reaction to her emotion. 'What could you have done?'

'We would probably have stayed on. Dardy offered to buy the farm to clear the debt, and he would have rented it back to us with the first two years of the lease free. After that the rent would have been something around seventy pounds a month.'

'Like the Murdons!'

David's head spun as he tried to fit the pieces of information together. It was like trying to make a jigsaw picture with only a few of the pieces.

20

Hey, Mane, This is Cool

Christmas came to Glenfune and David and Batt made the most of it. Just before Christmas a card arrived from David's father. On it he had written, 'Greetings to you and the old fellow. Keep your spirits up. I'm hoping to bring you home late in the spring or early summer.'

David showed the card to Batt.

'H-m-m!' Batt said. 'There's hope for us yet. Greetings to the old fellow is a big step forward.'

David asked Batt if he could have Ruction out for a visit during the Christmas holidays.

'Moriarty? Moriarty?' Batt puzzled, screwing up his eyes as he tried to remember where he had heard the name before. Then it struck him.

'Would his father be a garda?' he asked.

'That's right,' David said. 'His father is Garda Sorley Moriarty.'

'I knew him,' Batt said. 'He used to come out here before, counting the livestock. A good man. I had a lot of time for Moriarty.'

'Can I ask Ruction out then?'

'Of course you can. Tell him he can stay the night, or two nights, if he wants. The days are short this time of year.'

On the first afternoon of his stay Ruction was given tourist treatment. They stood on the rampart and David showed him the hill and the glen. The highlight should have been the lake and the water tumbling down from it, but Ruction took little interest. For him the most intriguing thing in Glenfune was the derelict house with broken windows, holes in the roof where slates had come loose, and were now lying smashed on the ground, and the crumbling plaster on the wall, great chunks of it fallen away to reveal the stone-work beneath.

Ruction couldn't keep his eyes off the broken-down house of Tim the Fiddler.

'What a scene!' he said, staring at it, and his mouth hung open in awe. 'In there the old guy bit the dust.'

'I wouldn't mind knowing exactly what happened there,' David said.

'Why don't we move in and have a gander?' Ruction said. 'We might turn up, like, clues or something.'

'We can't,' David said. 'The Murdons own it now. Anyway what could be there after fifteen years?"

'But Murdons don't have to know,' Ruction said, smiling archly.

'They could see us from their own house. Look. We can see it from here.'

'But could they see us when the lights are out?'

'You're talking about going down there after dark,' David said, 'and sneaking in like burglars.'

'Hey, mane, you catch on fast.'

'No! Not on, Ruction. What would your father say if he heard we broke into a house?'

'My old man doesn't need to know. Does he have to know?' Ruction asked. 'Anyway, look at the door. I bet that wouldn't keep out much. We just go in to take a gander. Make sure everything is in right nick.'

'We don't have a torch.'

'We do – my bike lamp.'

'Naw! I don't think so.'

But Ruction was fired up and didn't stop until he had persuaded David.

That night they just told Batt they were heading out for a walk and they went straight to the derelict house, going through the open gateway. The gate itself was gone, probably sold to scrap merchants. They stood still and listened. No sound but their own breathing. Murdons' dog barked and a sheep bleated high on the hill. Again silence and dark all around except for a rectangle of pale yellow light that was Murdons' window.

Ruction led the way to the door, looking right and left, and they had to persuade themselves that bushes standing in the nearby field were not people. Ruction jumped as something fluttered in a furze bush that leaned across the yard wall.

'A rat or a thrush having a nightmare,' David whispered to re-assure him.

Ruction pushed open the front door. It was stiff and creaked like a door in a spooky movie. To David it sounded loud enough to wake the dead. They stood still, waiting to make sure that no one else had heard it. There was only the sound of the night, an emptiness like the hush of faraway oceans in a seashell.

They went on tiptoe into the main room, a kitchen/living-room. It was dank with air that was trapped in the house from the time the last fire was lit there fifteen years earlier. The darkness indoors was total, as in a deep cave, so Ruction switched on the bike lamp.

David saw his friend's face, pale and shadowy in the glow of the lamp. Ruction was so caught up in the adventure that he reminded David of a cat eyeing a thrush on a lawn.

'Hey, mane, this is cool!' he whispered.

He let the beam of light rove around the room and picked out a few rickety chairs, a table, a bare dresser, all covered with a thick layer of powdery dust. Canisters, peat-brown with age and smoke, stood on a timber shelf above the fireplace, now a gaping hole as the range had gone the way of the gate.

Ruction took down the canisters and removed the covers, shining the lamp beam into them.

'What are you looking for?' David asked in a rough whisper. He was getting impatient with his companion. To Ruction it was all a bit of a lark. 'This isn't a storybook adventure, you know,' David said.

'I know,' Ruction whispered. 'This is a search and I'm looking for what's there. My dad says when you search a place, you don't poke around to find something special, just see what turns up.'

The canisters were empty.

They followed the beam of the lamp into a room off the kitchen. It had the remains of a bed, just the bed ends and a wire spring. Ruction dipped the light to the floor.

'Blood!' he whispered. 'Look! A dark patch. Blood!'

'You're nuts!' David said. 'I don't see anything.'

'This is it, mane,' Ruction said excitedly. 'This is where it happened.'

Ruction moved closer to the remains of the bed. Suddenly there was a loud crack, followed by a surprised yell from Ruction, as part of the floorboards collapsed beneath his feet.

'What are you trying to do?' David hissed. 'Are you trying to bring the Murdons in?'

'Ouch! My foot's stuck!' Ruction yelped.

'Would you shut up,' said David. ' You're OK. Just pull your foot out slowly.'

David took the lamp and shone it on the floor where Ruction was gingerly pulling his foot free of the broken floorboards.

'Come on,' David said. 'Let's get out of here.'

David switched off the lamp. 'Someone's coming!' he whispered.

They didn't move or make a sound as they listened to footsteps on the road. The steps came as far as the house and stopped. The two within stood frozen and waited for the steps to start walking again, hoping that whoever it was wouldn't come to check on the house. After what seemed like an age to them, the person on the road moved on up the glen.

'That's it,' said David. 'We've got to leave, now.'

'Wait!' Ruction said excitedly, 'There's something down here under the floorboards.'

David moved to his side, anxious to see what it was.

'It's papers,' Ruction said and he drew them out.

'Bring them with you. And come on!'

Before they went in home, David stowed the bundle of papers above the wall in the barn where the roof rafters came down to rest upon it.

'Nobody'll find them there,' he said.

The following day Ruction tried to get David to look at them, but David kept putting him off. He didn't want Ruction in on the search to find out who killed Tim the Fiddler. Only Josie knew he was doing that, and he wanted her to be there when he examined the find.

Ruction went home the following day. Batt told him to call out any time he wished.

'When the weather gets finer, you wouldn't miss it to jump up on your bike and come on out, and if you hadn't school the next day you could stay the night.'

It was clear that Batt had taken a liking to Ruction. It struck David that he had changed a lot from the man that greeted him with his back turned the first day he arrived in the glen. He had broken out of his solitude and talked a good bit more.

21

The Mystery of the Wandering Sheep

Ruction had no sooner gone than Josie came up to Batt's house.

'Guess what we found last night,' David said.

'I know. I met Ruction and he told me. Did you look at them?'

'Not yet. Come in. I'll get them. Batt's gone up the hill.'

They sat side by side at the table, their heads almost touching as they examined the mildewed papers, casting each aside as they saw that it was of little importance. Among them, however, was a passbook, and David watched as Josie eased the pages apart. It was difficult to read what was written because they were covered with brown stains and the ink was faded.

The last page was more legible than the rest, and they studied it closely. They saw a record of payments made monthly, but the most interesting things about it were the initials, which seemed to endorse each payment.

'I'll bet E.D. is Edward Dardy, or whatever his name is,' Josie said.

'Ewart,' David corrected her.

They spent a long time going over the figures, working things out on pages torn from the centre of one of David's exercise books.

'Just like Momma told us,' Josie said. 'Look! When he missed a payment he had to pay the interest anyway. Look at May and June.'

'Computer head!' David mocked. 'I'm lost.'

Josie worked quickly, scribbling figures, crossing them out again and writing new ones. David sat watching her.

'I have it now,' she said at last. 'The interest was three pence in the pound per month, just the same as it was for us.'

'I believe you,' David said, 'but look; it ends in November 1979, and Tim the Fiddler wasn't killed until the 19th of May in 1980.'

'I see that,' Josie said. 'And if Dardy had anything to do with it, I haven't a clue why he should kill the goose that was laying the golden eggs.'

'The people in the glen must have some idea about what happened,' David said. 'They were all questioned by the guards.'

'I'll ask Momma about it,' Josie said. 'She'd tell me more than Dad.'

✝ ✝ ✝

'You were right,' Josie said when they were coming home from school next day. 'The guards did question everyone in the glen.'

'I thought they would,' David said. 'Go on, tell me about it.'

Josie told him the story as she got it from her mother. It was a tale of comings and goings involving Batt and Mary and Pete Murdon.

'It's beginning to make sense for me now,' David said. 'I think I have the answer.'

'Go on, Sherlock. You're the detective.'

'OK,' David said. This is what I think happened. On the Monday – that was the 19th of May – Batt went to Tim the Fiddler and offered to buy his farm.'

Josie butted in right away: 'Nobody said he was trying to buy the farm.'

'Batt told the guards that he made a deal to buy the farm. I believe he tried to make the deal that evening but didn't finish it. Maybe the Fiddler was holding out for more money, or he

109

wanted to hang on to the house or something.'

'How do you know they didn't finish it?'

'Because Batt went down again on the Tuesday evening and spent a long time there. I know that was when they clinched the deal. Batt said so to the guards.'

David closed his eyes to concentrate on what he was saying.

'Batt had no sooner gone home,' he continued, 'than Mary Murdon called down to the Fiddler's house. Remember they were good friends. Mary brought him his dinner every day.'

'I know.'

'So, the Fiddler told her about Batt's offer. Next thing she dresses up and takes off on her bike, into town. To Dardy!'

'Sorry, David. You don't know that.'

'Who else in Coombowler would be interested in what was going on in Tim the Fiddler's farm? Tell me that.'

'OK. Maybe so. But why should Mary Murdon be in such a hurry to tell him about it?'

'Because Dardy had the Murdons across a barrel. For all we know, he might have told them to keep an eye on Tim the Fiddler. Maybe that's why Mary was so busy bringing him his dinner, and looking after him, and not out of the goodness of her heart. I think Dardy could get them to do anything. Anything! You know what I mean?'

Josie looked at him with two wide eyes.

'No!' she said, and her mouth stayed open in shock.

'I think "yes", Josie. Next day Pete Murdon goes up the hill, cuts the fence and drives the sheep through the gap. He comes down and tells Batt about his wandering sheep, and, when Batt goes up to look after them, Pete nicks the slasher. That night Pete or Mary go to Tim's house and —'

'Stop! I don't want to hear it.'

'Okay if you don't.'

'One problem with your story, Davy. Pete wouldn't be clever enough to think up those things. You know yourself he wanders in and out of the real world and keeps forgetting things.'

'I know he wouldn't be clever enough, but Mary would, and she controls him like a puppet. He depends on her for everything, even the words that come out of his mouth.'

'OK. So what are you going to do now?'

'I don't know.'

'What about Guard Moriarty? The guards are the ones to dig out information.'

'I can't,' David said.

'Why not?'

'Ruction! It was he found the stuff. If his father hears about it, he'll skin him alive.'

'You don't have to tell him Ruction was in on it.'

David wasn't sure about that.

'I'll have to sort it out with Ruction first,' he said.

22

He's a Cop, even in his Sleep

The Christmas holidays were over and school was in full swing. 'I want to let your dad in on what we found at the Fiddler's,' David said to Ruction.

'Why?'

'Something there he should know about.'

'No, mane. No way! You do that, I'm dead. See?'

'He doesn't have to know you were there.'

Ruction shook his head. 'No, Davy. You tell him, he'll know. He's kind of psychic. He's a cop, even in his sleep.'

'I'll lie to him if I have to.'

'No way!'

David changed tack. 'Ruction, I have to. It means a lot to me.'

Ruction paused. 'A lot?' he asked.

'Yes. Life and death.'

'Oh, God!' Ruction sounded desperate. He walked away from David towards the door into the school. He turned back and said, 'OK. I know you, mane. You're not going to lie if he asks the question.'

'No, but I won't tell him. I promise.'

'OK, mane. Go ahead. If it means that much to you, go ahead. Yes. Go ahead.'

And Ruction's shoulders slumped and his head was lowered as he made his way towards the locker-room door.

✝ ✝ ✝

Sorley Moriarty was like part of the town architecture, always there when you looked. Locals couldn't visualise the place without his presence. So David wasn't surprised when one day the Ford Mondeo with the garda sign on the roof slid noiselessly to the kerb just ahead of him.

'Hop in,' Sorley greeted him. 'You've something you want to show me?'

'Have I?' David said, still unsure of his ground.

'You have. Something yourself and that brat of mine found in Tim the Fiddler's place.'

'Oh!'

'Don't worry, boy. He told me you wanted to see me and I got the whole story out of him.'

'Don't blame him,' David said. 'It was all my fault.'

'That's funny. He said it was all his fault. And I believe him, because that's the kind of genius he is.'

'Were you mad with him?'

'Not that you'd notice. But he's going to be a model student for the next month or two with a lot of time for study, and he might be a bit hard up for cash.'

'I'm sorry. I'm really the one to blame.'

'All right, boy. Friendship is a fine thing to see, but lessons have to be learned, sometimes the hard way.'

David sat there, saying nothing.

'Cheer up, lad,' the garda consoled him. 'It's only a temporary hitch. Give it a month or two and the two of you will be laughing about it. Now, what was it you wanted to show me?'

'It's a passbook. I'll bring it in tomorrow.'

'Don't bother. I'll go out that way just for a visit, and we'll talk a bit more about it. Run away back to school now or you'll be late.'

The white Ford Mondeo with the garda sign on the roof caused a stir when it rolled sedately into the glen. Mary Murdon stood at her door and eyed it anxiously as it moved along the glen road. Julie Farren wondered when she saw it turn into Quilty's lane and glide over the rampart on its way to Batt's house.

'What brings you?' Batt asked when Sorley Moriarty came in the front door.

'Hadn't a whole lot better to do,' Sorley said. 'I thought I'd make a visit, and anyway, I wanted to say thanks for having my young fellow out during the Christmas.'

'You have a good young lad there,' Batt said. 'He's more than welcome.'

'He's not so bad. Like us all he has his good days and his bad days.'

They talked about old times, and about the changes that had taken place in such a short span of years and the ups and downs of sheep farming.

'I think I'll go east and have a look at the waterfall,' Sorley said to bring his visit to an end. 'It must be a mighty sight after all that rain.'

He spoke to David. 'Would you like to come along for the spin, David. I can drop you on the way back.'

✢ ✢ ✢

David had the passbook in his pocket, but he didn't mention it. He waited for the garda to say something about it. But Sorley was driving slowly, and he kept turning his head from side to side, admiring the glen and the hills that looked like hump-backed camels marching east.

He parked the car on the tourists' viewing platform at the head of the valley, and they sat there gazing at the skeins of white water cascading from a sharp edge of rock high on the hill. They listened to the thunder as it drummed up a fine mist over the pool that was gouged out of the rock at its foot.

After about ten minutes the garda broke the silence.

'Have you got it?' he asked.

David handed him the passbook and Sorley was quiet and focused as he ran his finger down the page and studied the message in the fading ink.

'You know what you have here?' he asked.

'I do,' David said, 'a moneylender's book. And he told him what Josie had discovered about the rate of interest and the repayments.

'What do you think?' David asked him.

'Before I tell you what I think, I must get your word that not one hint of this nor of anything I tell you about it will be breathed to another living soul.'

'What about Josie Farren?' David asked. 'She's been in it with me from the start.'

'No!' Sorley was adamant. 'Nobody. I must have your word. I wouldn't be telling you at all only for the abuse they flung at you in the school, and our Barry in the thick of it.'

'OK,' David said reluctantly. 'You have my word.'

'First of all I have to get the Superintendent's OK to reopen the Tim the Fiddler file. I'll see you around the town and I'll keep you up to speed from time to time.'

'The Tim the Fiddler file?' David asked.

'Yes. I have enough here to get Dardy for illegal money-lending, but I'm thinking it might lead to bigger things. It might be the piece of the jigsaw that was missing in the Fiddler case.'

'How come you didn't do something about the money lending before?' David asked. 'You knew about it.'

'The ones he swindled were like clams. They wouldn't talk, out of shame. That's why this little book is precious.'

Back at Quilty's lane, David got out and slammed the car

door. Sorley lowered the window and said, 'Remember. Not a word to a soul.'

23

Watching their Flock by Night

In the third week in February Agatha Christie sent for David. She told him that his grandfather had called. David would be needed at home for about a week. She spoke in her calm, matter-of-fact way, and it was hard to know whether she approved or disapproved. She suggested that he should keep in touch with schoolwork through Josie Farren.

'Your grandfather will meet you in Nunan's café,' she told him.

'What's up?' David asked when he joined Batt at a table in the café.

'Lambing,' Batt said. 'I was up the hill this morning and I found one of the ewes had dropped a lamb.'

'Oh, what does that mean?' David asked.

'It means that lambing time has come early, a week or more sooner than I had worked out.'

'OK, but why do you want me at home for a whole week?' David didn't understand.

'I thought it would be nice if you were around when the miracle is happening.'

'What miracle?' David asked, though he knew what Batt meant. He liked to pretend sometimes that he wasn't as tuned in to life on the farm as Batt wanted him to be.

'The miracle of birth,' Batt said. 'The miracle of new life coming into the world.' He glanced at David. 'We can be grieving for ever about the sadness of things dying, but there's always the miracle of birth.'

David was unmoved by Batt's enthusiasm, but he was curious as to what his own part in the arrival of new life would be. He didn't ask. He knew he wouldn't get an answer.

'Be patient,' Batt would say. 'You'll see.'

They had a meal in the café.

'It will save us having to get it when we go home,' Batt said. 'We'll have a few things to do.'

When they did get home, Batt checked the fence surrounding the sheepfold. David was given the job of collecting all the kindling he could find, withered gorse and heather, twigs from the birches that stood on the west side of the haggard, chips that had fallen near the chopping block. He brought them to the shelter in the sheepfold. Then he drew turf from the stack in the haggard and heaped it in a small stack beside the shelter.

'Are you going to burn it down?' he asked Batt, laughing.

'Funny man!' Batt said. 'You'll know in the middle of the night. Look at the sky; not a cloud, and it's going to stay fine for a spell. We'll have a clear, starry night and frost hard enough to go right into your bones.'

'You mean we're going to be out here at night?' David was astonished.

'Well, I will anyway. You make up your own mind about it.'

'But why?' David asked. 'What will we be doing out here?'

'We'll be helping them with the birthing if they need us.'

'Oh!' David said, and once again he didn't ask. He knew he would have to wait and see.

✢ ✢ ✢

Next morning they took Homer to the hill and drove the flock down to the sheepfold. They threw bales of hay here and there and scattered turnips about the fold. Batt told David to draw water from the well, to fill the concrete drinking-trough at the side of the fold and to keep it full until the sheep went back to the hill.

There, to a chorus of gentle bleating, the lambs were born. David was wide-eyed as he watched them arrive. Batt walked among the flock, and for the most part, his help was not needed. The birth just happened. But now and then there were problems. Then Batt helped to right the lamb so the head and forelegs came out first.

'Watch what I'm doing, Davy,' he said. 'You wouldn't know when you might have to do it yourself.'

Batt filled a gripsack in the kitchen and brought it to the shelter. He put in a flask of tea and some sandwiches, and four or five large lemonade bottles full of milk. Each bottle had a baby's-bottle teat tied firmly to its mouth.

'What are they for?' David asked.

'You'll see.'

As night came down, they built a fire before the shelter. They sat on the stone seat, their heavy coats draped across their shoulders, and they listened to the bleating of the ewes.

✛ ✛ ✛

Batt looked steadily into the fire, gazing at the glowing embers, and his eyes were like two sparks reflecting their light. Then he raised his head and said, 'Time to take a look,' and he put his arms into the sleeves of his coat, took the flashlight and moved off into the dark. David tracked his progress by the beam of the flashlight swinging from side to side, showing up the woolly bodies, lying down or shifting about. At the far corner of the fold the lamp was placed on the ground and Batt crouched over something. When he came back to the fire, he was carrying a tiny lamb in his arms.

'What's wrong?' David asked.

'This little one's mother doesn't want to know her,' Batt said.

'You're joking!'

'It happens.' Batt handed the lamb to David.

David held it in his lap and watched in sadness as it twisted its neck around, its mouth searching for food. Batt took a bottle of milk from the gripsack and handed it to David.

'Here, you feed it,' he said.

'How?'

'Just give it the teat. It has more sense than you. It'll know what to do.'

David put the teat to its mouth, and the lamb found it at once and began to guzzle the milk. Afterwards it lay on the ground beside David's feet and slept.

Batt put more turf on the fire and it flared up for a moment. David saw the sheeps' eyes shining like fireflies in the darkness beyond. Batt filled cups from the flask and they drank hot, sweet tea.

'I know who killed Tim the Fiddler,' David blurted out suddenly.

Batt laughed. 'That wouldn't surprise me at all,' he said. 'I told you before that some day you'll meet yourself coming back.'

'It was Pete Murdon, wasn't it?'

Batt said nothing, just gazed into the fire for a while, then looked around at the sheep and towards the Murdon farm to the west.

'You could be right,' he said softly.

'And you did nothing about it?' David said in amazement. 'You knew about it and you did nothing.'

'What do you think I should have done?' Batt spoke calmly.

'Told the guards all you knew. Simple enough.'

'And what would have happened then?'

'Pete Murdon would have been arrested and your name would be cleared.'

'And what would have happened to poor old Pete?'

David hadn't been thinking of the possible outcome for Pete. 'I don't know,' he said.

'Well then, let me draw a picture for you,' Batt said, and he poked at the fire with a length of stick. 'Imagine Pete standing inside the fence near the house when a car arrives. Two guards get out and they ask him to come with them to the barracks. He stands there looking at them and wondering what's going on. Mary runs out of the house and begs the guards not to take him away.

'Pete is dumbstruck. His poor old scrambled brain can make neither head nor tail of it. What happened before is drowned in the great lake of forgetting that he has instead of a memory. He goes away with them like a lamb going to the mart, and, like the lamb, he won't be coming back, but he doesn't know that.

'They'll find him guilty and he'll spend the rest of his life in some place with grey walls and no sun. I don't know if he'll remember what it was like while he was living in Glenfune, but sometimes he's bound to wonder where his hill is gone, why he never strolls out in the morning and goes through the fields with the dog dancing around him with glee just for being alive and being there.

'No, the poor old creature will be lost in a muddle of mind pictures and be bored out of his brains. Ah, yes, maybe he struck the blow, but he was no more guilty than if he was a rag doll. There was another hand guiding the slasher.'

'Whose hand?'

'I'd say you have a good idea because you're a smart lad.'

David was speechless for a while. At length he said softly, 'But what about you, Grandad?'

'There was no fear of me.'

The sky was full of stars, and it was very cold outside the circle of firelight. The first sign of day came from a human source; a light went on in Farrens'. It was followed soon by a light in the high dormer window in Murdons' house.

'You should go in and light the fire in the range,' Batt said. 'Put on the porridge and we'll have a bit of breakfast.'

'Can I stay here for another bit?' David asked. 'I want to see the daylight coming in over Farrens' hill.'

'All right. There's a drop of tea in the flask. We might as well have it.'

They sat drinking tea and they let the fire dwindle to a few red embers, glowing ever more faintly as day brightened. Gradually sheep and hills and bushes, and the hurdles surrounding the sheepfold and the outcropping grey stone took shape as the hill and the glen came out of the darkness.

24

The Devil-Bird Swoops

David jumped to his feet in alarm when Batt roared. The old man shot out of the seat and ran towards the fence. He picked up a stone and hurled it, shouting, 'Go to hell, you black devil!' Startled sheep scattered before him as he charged through the flock.

The black bird, perched on a fence post, ignored the crazy human running towards him, arms awhirl. But when a stone clattered against its perch, it turned its black head, flapped its wings, rose into the air, and flew lazily to a new perch on the gallaun in the haggard.

'It's one of those two-coloured crows,' David said when Batt came back to the shelter. 'They're all over the place.'

'Bloody scald crow,' Batt spat out the words.

'Why did you drive it off?' David asked.

'They attack the lambs if they can get them on their own.'

'Would they kill them?'

'It happens.'

David called his pet lamb Sheba. When he went into the house to cook the porridge for breakfast, the lamb followed him. He fed her again.

Throughout the day he and Batt took turns in the sheepfold. If David saw a ewe in trouble, he was to call Batt. However, when it did happen Batt had gone down to the meadow in the lowland to fetch the goats. He was out of earshot, and David decided to try it on his own.

He had seen Batt do it, and he tried to do exactly the same thing. He pushed gently and probed until he found the leg that was turned under. He eased it forward, then stepped back and watched the lamb come into the world. He yelled with delight when he saw the little thing get to its feet, stagger, fall, and rise again. At that very moment Batt arrived back in the sheepfold.

'I did it,' David was delighted. 'That one there was turned the wrong way and I righted it.'

Batt looked at the lamb, then at David.

'Well done, Davy!' he said at last, quietly, as if he couldn't believe it.

All day, in and out of the house, David's lamb followed him. By nightfall they were feeding four abandoned ones, but only David's hankered after human company. It snuggled up to him whenever he sat down, and he stroked it and tickled its ears as if it were a pup.

As night was falling, they lit the fire before the shelter and settled down for the night watch. The sky was clear and soon filled with stars. It was cold away from the fire, but in the shelter it was cosy. Not alone did they have the heat from the fire, but, when it was burning for a while, the stones at the back of the shelter grew less cold.

Batt and David recited the twenty-third psalm together, as they had done every evening since David arrived in Knocklee. David had come to like it, its quaint words and pleasing rhythms. He hadn't bothered too much about what it meant, being satisfied with just the vague notions it stirred in his mind.

'He restoreth my soul,' David said. 'What's that about?'

'Your namesake, King David, wrote the psalms. Shepherding out there in the east where King David was living is not the same as it is here,' Batt said. 'When the flock goes out of the sheepfold in the morning, it strings out in a line, and the sheep stay in the same place in the line for the whole day.

'But every one of those sheep, at some time during the day, will leave the line and go to the shepherd. The shepherd will fondle the sheep, like you are doing there with that lamb, bending down and whispering words into its ear, and the sheep will rub up against his legs and nibble at his ear and that sort of thing. Then the sheep goes back into its place in the line.'

'What words does he say when he whispers?' David asked. 'Do you know them?'

'Not really. I just have an idea that they'd be words of friendship and love — petting words. Anyway the sheep goes back to the line and it's happy. That's what the psalm is talking about: "He restoreth my soul."'

David thought about it for a while.

'What's the point of talking to them,' he said, 'when they can't understand a word he says?'

'How do you know they can't?' Batt said. 'All the meaning isn't in the words alone. You can convey a lot in the way you say things. Look at that little one there. She's as happy as can be listening to you cooing at her and telling her she's good, and that you'll take care of her. She doesn't have to know what it means. There's an awful lot of sense in the way you say it.'

Batt took the torch and followed its beam through the flock. David put more turf on the fire and drew his coat close about him. He whispered the psalm to himself again.

'All is quiet,' Batt said when he returned and sat down beside David.

✟ ✟ ✟

The night went by peacefully, and in the morning David went to the house to get the breakfast ready. At the same time, Batt went to the haggard to bring more bales of hay to the fold. As David stirred the porridge, he heard Batt yelling. He dropped the spoon and rushed out of the house.

Batt was standing beside the ashes of the fire, a lamb in his arms. It was Sheba. David knew her, even though all lambs are very much alike at that stage. He looked at Batt, and saw his eyes shining with tears.

'What is it?' David asked, and then he saw the lamb's eyes.

It would be more correct to say that he didn't see the lamb's eyes. The lamb didn't have eyes. Tiny trickles of blood ran from the corners of the eye sockets, but there were no eyes. David stood in a state of horror, staring and his mouth hanging open.

'A bloody scald crow!' Batt said. 'I was gone to the haggard only a few minutes and the devil-bird swooped on the little thing.'

David found his voice. At first he said no word, just let out a roar that was a mixture of anger and horror and grief. He looked at Batt.

'You shouldn't have left her!' he shouted. 'The hay could have waited. I thought one of us was to be with them all the time!'

Then he ran. He didn't care where once he was running. He headed for the hill, and Batt watched him grow smaller as he charged up towards the lake. At the lake he strode crazily over and back across the gravel shore, scarcely knowing what he was doing. He picked up stones and threw them viciously into the water. He threw one so fiercely that it flew over the water and struck the face of the cliff beyond the lake. That made him stop. It wasn't possible to throw a stone that far, but he had done it.

He calmed down then, but he felt as if the weight of the world's sorrows were loaded on his back. He walked back down the hill, passed through the sheepfold without speaking and went into the house. Batt followed him and found him sitting on a chair before the range, a dazed look on his face.

'You should go up to the bed and take a rest,' Batt said. 'You've been up for two nights now with hardly any sleep. You must be dead tired.'

'I'm OK,' David said, and there was no life in his voice.

'I'll have to get back to them,' Batt said. 'Take my advice and go on to bed. I'll call you later.'

As he was going out the door, David raised his head and asked: 'What about Sheba?'

'I'll take care of her.'

'You're going to kill her, aren't you?'

'Would you prefer if she lived on, the way she is, and watch her suffer and fade away or be savaged by foxes and ravens?'

'No,' David said weakly.

When Batt had gone back to the sheepfold, David felt tiredness take over. He stood up and climbed the stairs. His feet felt like two bags of lead. When he reached the bed, he flopped down on it. But he didn't go to sleep.

✛ ✛ ✛

It was cold outside the bedclothes, so David threw off his boots and crept underneath. Gradually warmth spread over his body, right down to his toes. He dropped into a dream – you couldn't call it sleep, for his mind was a jumble of flying things: the eyeless lamb – the scald crow, with eyes on fire, hovering above the lamb, its beak open, screeching – Batt's sad eyes downcast over the helpless lamb – Fred Dardy's sneering look – a rabble of grotesque people with hideous mouths open, bleating like sheep – baa-baa-baa.

And then he saw his mother's face, full of pain, as she looked up at him from the stretcher for the last time – then again Batt plodding up the hill to look after his sheep – the lamb – the scald crow – the bleating monsters advancing, then retreating, and, as the whirling images slowed and his mind grew quiet, his

127

mother's face was there again, but now it was serene and that half smile that was her usual expression softened and spread into a loving glance, and his heart was too full to resist his tears, and they came tumbling from his eyes and ran down his cheeks.

He cried as he had never cried. Great sobs shook his body. He was crying for many things: for Batt, for the lonely life the old man led, for the ridicule he endured with patience; he cried for his own father, for his desolation after Mom's death; he cried for Mom who was given such a short time to be alive; and he cried for himself.

Through his tears he saw Batt standing at the door of the bedroom. He tried to stop crying, but he couldn't. Batt came to the bedside and laid his hand on David's head. 'Have your cry, Davy,' he said. 'It will do you good.'

Then Batt left the room and the house and went back to the sheepfold.

For David the sobbing and the crying stopped, though the sadness stayed with him. But it was different. It no longer scalded his heart. It had changed to a sadness that was in harmony with the music of life, and he could live with it.

Sleep descended on him like a healing balm, and when he woke again it was night. The heavens were full of stars, so bright in the frosty sky that they looked like points of silver fire. He got out of bed and went to the back window. The fire glowed in the sheepfold, and Batt sat beside it, his head bent as he gazed into its flames.

David switched on the light. He put on his boots and turned to go downstairs. His eye fell on the picture of his mother, still turned face down on the bedside locker. For a long time he stared at the back of the picture. Finally he turned it over and looked at her. The pain and rage that he had known when he first saw it was not there now. Then she had seemed remote, as if she had deserted him. Now she seemed closer, and the half smile on her face could be directed at himself. He put the picture standing on the locker, facing towards the door so that he could see it when he entered the room. Downstairs he put on his overcoat and went out to the sheepfold. Batt looked up when he heard his footsteps.

'Are you all right?' he asked.

'Yeah. I'm OK,' David said, and he sat down beside Batt on the stone seat. They were silent for a long time, their heads lowered, looking into the dancing flames.

'Did she ever sit out here with you at lambing time?' David asked after a while.

Batt looked up quickly. 'Who? Your mother?' he asked.

'Yes.'

'No. She didn't. But she brought us the tea and something to eat in the middle of the night.'

'Did she like doing it?'

'I think she did. She looked after the orphans too. She brought them in and fed them, and kept them there until they were ready to stand on their own feet.'

'They were safe from the scald crows then,' David said.

'They were.'

They were quiet again for a while. Batt broke the silence.

'Did you like being here?' he asked.

'Oh, yes. Even though we lost Sheba, it was great anyway. Magic!'

✝   ✝   ✝

As the lambs gained strength, they and their mothers were let into the lowland meadows to feed well on the good grass before they returned to the rougher fare of the hill. After a few weeks the sheepfold was abandoned. It was bare of grass, just a paddock of brown earth.

'Is it ruined?' David asked.

'No,' Batt assured him. 'It will green up again in no time. I might scatter a bit of seed on it just to hurry it up.'

25

Sorley on the Case

David was dawdling down Main Street, looking around as if he were trying to pick out a face in the crowd. He was alone, acting on a message from Garda Sorley Moriarty.

'What's going on with you and my da?' Ruction had asked him.

David was taken aback. Had Ruction's father discussed the Tim the Fiddler affair with his son?

'What do you mean?' David asked, playing for time.

'He said he wanted to talk to you. In private!'

'Oh,' David said, and he relaxed. 'When?'

'There's something weird about this, mane. He said if you go down Main Street at lunch hour today, he'll see you.'

The garda car was parked between a Hi-Ace van and an expensive-looking Mercedes with a ball hitch. When David drew level, its headlights flashed, and he saw Garda Moriarty in the driving seat, beckoning to him.

'Some progress in that business,' he said when David sat in.

'Yes?'

'Yes. Good news and bad. The good news is we know who did it. The bad news is he got away.'

'Got away?' David exclaimed. 'I saw Pete yesterday. He's still in the glen.'

'You have it pinned on the wrong man. Pete didn't do it.'

'But Batt thinks he did.'

'Jumping to conclusions,' Sorley said, 'like our own crowd.'

'All right, then! Who did it?' David asked, bursting to know the truth.

'I'll tell you if you'll listen.'

'I'm listening,' David said.

'When I got to read the file,' Sorley began,' I knew that the first one I had to question was Mary Murdon. The Murdons were too damn close to the thing for comfort.'

'You didn't come to the glen. Nobody said you were there.'

'No. I met her in Tubber. I found out at the post office that she did her shopping on a Friday.'

And Sorley told his story.

✦ ✦ ✦

Questioning Mary Murdon had been like trying to open a can of beans with a lollipop stick, but he had managed.

'In the beginning I just tried to sow a few seeds of panic. I looked her between the eyes and said, "Tim the Fiddler". Nothing else. Just "Tim the Fiddler".'

That rattled her. She looked this way and that way, and he could almost hear her thinking: 'What's he at? Tim the Fiddler is dead. It's over. Why is he raising it now? How much does this fellow know?' Sorley just stood there and waited. That's where the patience comes in, he told David. Give them time enough to worry. But that one was a tough lady.

'What about Tim the Fiddler?' she says, cool as you like.

He let her stew for a while. In the end she asked him again, 'Well, what about him?'

He knew then that he had her on the run.

'Pete,' he said and waited.

He could see her swallowing and she was staring at him, probably trying to get an idea of what he was thinking.

'Pete had nothing to do with it,' she said.

He looked down at the ground. Technique again, giving

them the idea you don't really want to say what you're going to say.

'The slasher!' he said. He still hadn't asked a question. Just kept throwing words at her. Words with a lot of meaning hanging on to them. Harmless enough in the beginning, but getting like whiplashes as they went on. He could see the fright coming into her eyes.

'The slasher?' she says, but he said nothing, just kept looking at the ground.

'Pete didn't go near the slasher,' she said.

He said nothing, and she kept looking around her as if she was hoping that she might see something that would put an end to Moriarty's probing.

He looked at her again, straight in the eye. Not a word out of him for a while. And then he hit her with the big shot.

'Dardy!' says he.

She looked like she had a pain, and he felt sorry for her. She didn't know what to say. She turned on her heel and walked away from him. 'I've had enough of this,' she said.

'Dardy might like to sing a song,' he called after her.

She stopped and stood with her back to him.

'Dardy is the greatest liar since Aesop,' she said, and she got on her bike and rode away.

Straight away he went into town and called on Dardy. Here the technique had to be different, 'because Dardy was what you might call a substantial citizen'. Sorley told him that he was investigating illegal money-lending in Coombowler and 'the area in its vicinity'.

Dardy wanted to know why Garda Moriarty came to him. He knew nothing about money-lending, legal or otherwise. Sorley told him that he had just had a word with Mary Murdon, and that set off the alarm bells in the shopkeeper's brain. He didn't

133

care what Mary Murdon said, it was a barefaced lie.

'She didn't lie to me,' Sorley said.

'What did she say?' Dardy asked.

'It doesn't matter. More important is what you're going to say.'

'Are you going to bring me in, Guard Moriarty?'

'Not now, Mr Dardy. Not yet. But be around for a while and I'll see what I can do!'

'And I left him standing there in his upstairs sitting-room, looking at my back and I going out the door. He threw some tough words after me that I wouldn't like to repeat.'

'But you had nothing to go on yet,' David said

'No, though I had stirred the pot. I thought you were going to listen to me.'

'I am. Sorry!'

Sorley went on with the story. When he left Dardy's, he drove straight to Glenfune and parked out of sight behind Tim the Fiddler's. Mary Murdon was standing at their gate, peering into the dark. She had seen the lights of a car shining briefly on the ceiling and was wondering whose car it was and where it had got to.

She jumped when Sorley appeared suddenly out of the night.

'You again!' she said. 'What are you after now?'

'Unless I'm very much mistaken, ' Sorley said, 'you're going to have a visitor.'

'What? Who?'

'Dardy!'

'What does he want?'

'I don't rightly know, but I have a feeling that he might be trying to pin some bad deeds on you and Pete.'

Her face turned red. She shook like an aspen, and tore at her hair.

'That sneaky snake!' she shouted. 'He's the one himself. He's the one who did it.'

And the story poured out of her. She wasn't proud of the part they had played in it, but Dardy had them in a stranglehold on account of money they owed him. When Mary found out that Tim the Fiddler was going to sell-out to Batt Andy, she went into town and tipped him off. He persuaded them to rob Batt's slasher, and he came out to Glenfune in the dead of night and took the slasher with him down to Tim's. Poor old Tim was found the next morning.

'So it was Dardy!' David was excited. 'I was sure it was Pete.'

'A lot of people were. I always had my doubts. Pete is a gentle soul. I couldn't see him doing it.'

'What happened then?'

'Dardy arrived in Glenfune, just like I thought he would. Mary opened the door and let him in. He got one hell of a shock when he saw me there. I stood up and began to say my piece; you know, the usual rigmarole: "I'm arresting you, Mr Dardy, on suspicion of murder. It is my duty to warn you – and before I could say another word, he was gone, out the door, into the car, and off.'

'You followed him?'

'Yes, but I had to calm down Mary first. She was terrified that Dardy would come back for her. By the time I got to the house, it was empty, no sign of man, woman or child. Everyone gone. Now we think they must have left the country. Don't ask me how they did it, but that's what we think.'

'So, he's got away with it,' David said.

'For now. He'll be traced and brought back to stand trial. It might take a while, but he can't hide forever.'

'How come you didn't find that out fifteen years ago?' David asked, and he sounded angry.

'We didn't have the key to open it up. The key was the pass-book you found. And now it's time you were getting back to school if you don't want to be late.'

✛　✛　✛

Dardy's shop was closed for two weeks. Then a large poster appeared stuck to the inside of the window, obscuring the goods displayed there. In large red letters it announced:

CLOSING DOWN SALE

Then a few weeks later the shop was locked up, all goods removed from it, and an estate agent's notice appeared telling the world that 'this valuable property' was for sale. The Dardy family disappeared from Coombowler. It was a nine-day wonder. Several outrageous rumours about them ran like wildfire around the town, and then they faded into folklore.

26

There's a Car at Batt Andy's

One afternoon David and the Farrens walked home from the mouth of the glen. As they approached the Farren house, Josie said, 'There's a car at Batt Andy's.'

David looked up and saw it, perched on the rampart as if the driver were reluctant to approach the house. He recognised the car, a Mazda 626, dark green. It was his dad's car. He stood still. The others stood, waiting for him to say something.

'What is it?' Josie asked. 'Do you know who it is.'

'I do,' David answered, and he stood there with his mouth open in surprise.

'Who?'

'It's my dad, and I bet he's come to take me home.'

'Oh!'

'There's a woman walking around the car,' young Sally said.

'And there's a man in it,' Annie added.

David was speechless. This was a bolt from the blue. He hadn't been thinking of his father. And who was the woman? Mrs Branagan? Couldn't be. She would have gone into the house. No doubt his dad was waiting for David to arrive home from school.

Batt must have seen the car. Did he know who was in it? He must do. As always, Batt would wait for the other one to make the first move. He would have a good idea as to why his father had come.

This was an upheaval, no matter how you looked at it. David

had settled in to life in the glen. He and Batt had both fallen in to the routine of life on the farm and in school. Was David now to have to go through another change? And the most puzzling thing was the woman. Who was she, and what was she doing there?

'I'll have to go up and see what they want,' he said, so softly that he could have been speaking to himself.

He walked up the lane, his eyes fastened on the thin woman who walked around the car, looking about her, like a tourist taking in the sights. She stood with her back to him, gazing up at the water tumbling from the lake. She was so narrow, without substance, like one of those fashion models.

When she heard his footfall, she turned round and looked at him, a penetrating look. Although she had prominent cheekbones and intense grey eyes, she seemed pleasant enough. A smile broke the hard set of her features.

'You must be David,' she said in an English accent.

Her voice alerted his dad, seated in the driver's seat.

'Hey, David,' he said, and he hopped out of the car and embraced his son.

'Over the top as always,' David thought.

That was the great contrast between them. Mom was reserved. You had to guess how she felt about things. Whatever she said was understated, just like Batt.

'We've come to take you home, David,' his dad said. 'I'd say you've been long enough in this dump.'

'It's not a dump,' David said.

'Maybe not, but it doesn't come up to what you're used to at home in Woodbine Avenue. Eh?' He was seeking David's agreement, but the boy was silent.

'It's certainly different,' David said eventually.

His father chuckled, but the woman looked questioningly at

David. She seemed to have understood that he didn't share his father's opinion of Knocklee.

Her being there with his father carried overtones that David didn't want to think about. The thought that this skinny lady might be about to take his mother's place appalled him. Already he sensed that she was much sharper than his dad, and, knowing his dad as he did, he believed that she would run his life. That might be a good thing for Dad, but he had noticed her questioning look when he said that the two places were different.

'Who's she?' David asked his dad, as if she weren't there at all.

Her face reddened and her lips tightened. Rather than answer his question his father put an arm around his shoulders and said, 'Come for a little stroll with me. I have something I want to talk to you about.' He turned to the woman and said, 'Will you excuse us for a minute, Jacinta?'

His father turned as if to walk down the lane to the glen road.

'Let's walk towards the house,' David said. 'I might want to talk to Batt about things anyway.'

'Who?'

'Batt.'

'Oh, your grandfather. I'd prefer if that old – if he weren't involved just yet.'

'I think he has to be,' David said. 'Let's walk in that direction.'

'Oh all right. Have it your way,' John Lakes was peeved. 'I would have written to you,' he said, 'but I thought it might be better if I talked to you face to face. There's something very cold and formal about the written word. It's easy to take the wrong meaning out of something that's written down.'

'You're going to marry her, aren't you?' David said.

'God, you're very direct.'

'We don't beat about the bush.'

'Who's we?'

'Me and Batt.' David stopped and looked at his father. 'You *are* going to marry her, aren't you?' he repeated.

'Not going to, David. We're married already. Jacinta's your new mother now.'

'My mother is dead,' David said quietly, and his calm was more telling than if he had shouted at the top of his voice. His father was taken aback by his quiet tone.

'Well, you know what I mean, 'John Lakes blustered. 'She will be a mother to you in every way. She is a kind and gentle person, and you'll come to like her when you get to know her.'

✢ ✢ ✢

They had reached the door of the house. David opened it and went in. His father did not follow. Batt was sitting in a chair by the window, the light from outside brightening one side of his face.

'My dad is here,' David said.

'I thought it might be himself,' Batt said. 'And who's the woman?'

'She's his wife,' David said.

Batt went on as if he hadn't heard. 'What do they want?' he asked.

'They want to bring me home,' David told him.

'And what about you? Is that what you want too?'

'I don't know,' David said. 'I always thought I'd be going back home when Dad sorted things out.'

'You'll be going then?'

David hesitated. 'Do I have to go?' he asked. 'It's not like I thought it would be. It never came into my thoughts about Dad getting married again.'

John Lakes chose that moment to open the door and step into the kitchen. Batt looked at him without expression. He offered no word of welcome, or even recognition. There was a long silence.

'I've come to bring him home,' John Lakes said. 'I'm sure you'll be glad to get him off your hands.'

Batt didn't comment on that. 'How does he feel about it himself?' he asked.

'I want time to think about it,' David volunteered.

'What time do you want? There's nothing to think about,' his father said. 'You're coming home where you belong.'

'Oh, yes, there *is* something to think about.' David said. Still he didn't raise his voice. 'Some things have changed.'

'I know things have changed,' John Lakes said. 'But that's the way of life. Things are always changing, and we have to make the best of them.'

'I won't go with you today,' David said.

'You don't have a choice, boy,' his dad said. He never called him 'boy' except when he was angry with him. He was angry with him now because, obviously, he expected David to be delighted at the prospect of going home.

'I hope you haven't forgotten that I'm your father,' he said.

'I haven't,' David retorted, 'but I think you forgot you had a son.'

'He said he wants time to think,' Batt butted in. 'Another week or two won't make much difference.'

'No!' John Lakes stormed. 'He's been here long enough, too long! Now he's coming home.'

'Not yet,' David told him. 'I said I want to think about it.'

'You've got to come,' his dad insisted. 'There's nothing to think about. You don't have a choice.'

'What are you going to do about it?' Batt said. 'Put him in chains?'

'You stop encouraging him,' John Lakes bellowed, and he

141

pointed a finger at Batt. 'I'll have you arrested, you old codger. But that wouldn't be a new experience for you, would it?'

David said, 'I think you'd better go, Dad. I'll write to you and let you know what I decide.'

Batt stood up and moved towards the door.

'All right, then,' John Lakes said. 'I'll go!' He pointed at Batt again and said, 'You haven't heard the last of it!'

He marched to the door, and slammed it after him as he left.

David went out and watched his father go back to the car and speak to Jacinta. She reached out and caressed his cheek. They got into the car. Jacinta stood for a moment, looking back towards the house before she got in and closed the door. The car moved off down the lane. David listened to the drone of its engine growing faint as it moved along the glen.

'Do I have to go back?' he asked when he returned to the kitchen.

'You can stay in this house for as long as you want to,' Batt said. 'But it isn't up to me.'

'So who is it up to?' David asked.

'I think your father has rights over you more than anyone else.'

'What about me?' David was indignant. 'Have I no rights?'

'Not in a case like this, I think,' Batt said. 'I think you have to be a certain age before you can become independent. I don't know what age that is, but I'd say it's more than fourteen.'

✝ ✝ ✝

For the next few days David took to walking up to the lake and sitting on a flat rock on its shore. He pitched pebbles into the water and watched the ripples spread out from the splash.

He should be pleased that his dad was better and that he could go home. But the woman changed everything. Batt didn't speak about it. He wouldn't! David could imagine him saying, 'I

142

thought you'd prefer to work it out for yourself.'

'Is there something on your mind?' Josie asked him.

'Why do you ask?'

'Impossible to get a word out of you these days, and I've spotted that old faraway, daydreaming look in your eyes several times in class.'

'Yes, you're right,' David said. 'I have things on my mind. I'll tell you about it some time.'

27

Making-Up Time

David was having trouble with the word 'home'. He had begun to call the house in Knocklee 'home', but when his father said he would bring him 'home', he was speaking about the house in Cork. Their house in Woodbine Avenue would never again be home for him. It was going to be a place arranged and tended by a stranger's hands.

By degrees all traces of the real mother of the house would be gone. The new woman, Jacinta, would introduce some of her own things, buy new bits and pieces of furniture and things like curtains and carpets for it. She would rearrange the cupboards and shelves. This interloper, Jacinta, would busy herself, cleaning, tidying, dusting, and flitting from room to room, filling it with her presence, leaving her scent to claim it as her own.

The farm on Knocklee was more his place now. It was hallowed by his mother's footprints, the touch of her hands. It was the sight that met her eyes for much of her young life. It was the place that had made her what she was. David had a sense of having grown out of this grey hillside and the stone house where he had lived for almost a year, and he felt closer there to the woman who left it to bring him into the world.

He hadn't known his dad's people or his native place in the way that he knew this place. His dad seemed to have parted from his own family when he married, and David had never got to know them.

During the days that he waited for a decision about his future,

David walked every inch of the farm. Almost every day after school, when he had eaten his dinner, he walked up the hill, up to the lake, and on to the summit. He wanted to know every bit of it, because he knew that he would have to leave it before long.

✢ ✢ ✢

John Falvey, the solicitor, called to the house.

'I like to take a drive out this way,' he said when he came into the kitchen and sat by the table. 'The slightest excuse will do me.'

'What's your excuse this time, John?' Batt asked.

John Falvey turned to David. 'Your grandfather would get the Nobel Prize for small-talk,' he said, and he laughed. David laughed with him, and even Batt managed a smile.

John Falvey became serious.

'I've had a phone call from Matt Branagan,' he said. 'David's father asked him to start legal proceedings to have his son returned to his home.'

'What does that mean?' David asked.

'It means he wants a court order awarding him custody of you.'

'Any point in fighting it?' Batt asked.

'Hard to say. Considering his recent problems, there might be a chance, but it would be iffy.'

Nothing was said for a minute or two. Then John Falvey said, 'Matt Branagan thinks it would be better if you came to some agreement and avoided going to court. I think he's right.'

'What kind of agreement would that be?' Batt asked.

'I don't know. Something like David's father agreeing to let him come down here for visits, to spend some of his holidays here. That kind of thing.'

'I wouldn't stand in the way,' Batt said. 'I have nothing against John Lakes. The problem is that he doesn't think the world of me.'

'Well, you thought it was the Tim the Fiddler thing that had him upset. That's cleared up now.'

'Does he know that?' Batt asked.

'He does. Matt Branagan told him.'

'Well, if he's prepared to come down and talk about it, I don't mind,' Batt said.

'OK, then. I'll phone Matt Branagan when I go back and see can we arrange a meeting.'

✢ ✢ ✢

'The car is there again,' Josie said as they walked home two days later. The Farrens were much quicker than David to see things like that. The picture of the glen was so firmly imprinted on their minds that if the slightest thing were out of place, they would spot it immediately.

David was surprised to find only the woman, Jacinta, in the car.

'Where's my dad?' he asked by way of greeting.

'He's in Coombowler.'

'Why didn't he come?'

'I asked him not to,' Jacinta said, 'until I'd had a word with you.'

'A word about what?' David asked.

'About everything. I think I'm the problem for you. Isn't that so?'

David didn't answer.

'It's only natural,' she said. 'So I think it's a good idea if we have a talk before anything is decided.'

'OK.'

She was nobody's fool, David felt, probably straightforward and knowing. A bit like his mother in a way.

'I'm not trying to take your mother's place,' she said.

'Nobody can ever do that.'

'Then maybe I should be staying on here,' David said.

'That would hurt your dad very much. He has been looking forward for a long time to having you back. He spoke to me about you all the time.'

'He ignored me,' David said, 'as if I didn't exist. He went off to England and married you and I didn't know a thing about it.'

'Don't forget he was under a lot of pressure at that time. He was great to get over his problem, and he did it while he was holding down a tough job over there.'

'Is he all right now? You know what I mean,' David asked.

'You mean has he stopped drinking too much? Well, he has.'

'It doesn't matter what I say. He can force me to go back if he wants to.'

'And you don't want to go?'

'I do and I don't.'

She smiled at him. 'If I weren't there, you wouldn't have a problem. Is that it?'

'Sort of.'

'Why don't you give it a go for a while? I wouldn't try to be your mother – more like a relation spending some time with you and your dad. I think we could get along all right. I like the way you speak your mind.'

'You don't mess around either,' David said.

'You'll come home, then?'

'I don't know. Half of me wants to stay with Batt. I think you'd like Batt.'

'I think I might.'

'But if I went back, my dad would never let me come down here to visit.'

'He might if we could get the two of them to patch up their differences.'

'No trouble with Batt, but I don't know about my dad. He's very black about Batt.'

'Do you think we could talk him around?'

'You mean you and me?'

'Yes. I think it's up to us. Will you try with me?'

'Well. OK.'

They decided that David would put it to Batt, and she would go to Coombowler and talk to John. She sat into the car, saying, 'Give me a couple of hours, and I'll have him back here.'

As David had expected, Batt was agreeable. 'I have nothing against the man. He mightn't think for himself enough, but that's not a mortal sin. Foolish though.'

'Why did you try to come between him and my mother?' David asked.

'What's that?' Batt said, looking up, startled. 'Who said that?'

'He did in his letter to me. Something about you not liking people from towns.'

'Oh, that?' Batt said, and he lowered his gaze and stared at the floor for a while. After what seemed a long time to David, he spoke again.

'You have to understand what it's like to have your own piece of land, Davy.' Batt was speaking dreamily as if his words were slipping out from some secret place in his mind. David felt he was just eavesdropping on the man's thoughts. 'Here on this hill our family is free, free to do anything we damn well want to do, and no one can put in or out on us. From some time back in the roots of time a Quilty got a hold of this place and we have it since. Our fathers and grandfathers and all before them have walked the slopes of Knocklee in winter and summer and all kinds of weather, and whatever about anywhere else in the world, while we're on this hill we're kings.'

He paused, probably surprised at himself for making such a

long speech.

'I really don't get it,' David said.

'Well, is it any wonder that I didn't want it to go to some gligeen of a townie that would think nothing of throwing it away to the Murdons or Dardy or any loodheramawn that had the few pounds to buy it?'

He sat with downcast eyes in silence for a while as though regretting his outburst.

'Do you understand me?' he said in the end.

'I think so,' David said.

28

Picking Whortleberries

It was just short of two hours when David saw the car arrive on the crest of the rampart. Jacinta remained seated at the wheel, but John got out, walked around to the driver's side and talked excitedly to his wife. He walked up and down, shooting his hands about like a band conductor, and speaking in a loud voice. Batt and David watched at the window.

'I think you'd better go up there and see what's going on,' Batt said.

John turned to David when the boy got to the car.

'Do you know what she wants me to do?' he said. 'Go down there and shake hands with old Humanity Dick himself. No way. No way!'

'Why not?' David asked. 'Batt wouldn't mind, and he has more reason than you not to shake hands.'

'He has. Has he?'

'Yes. He has nothing to apologise for. You know he had nothing to do with the Tim the Fiddler business.'

'I know that, but don't you realise? We have been at war for years.'

'You were. He wasn't.'

John rested his hands on the bonnet of the car and stood there with his head raised to heaven. He was silent.

'Please, John,' Jacinta pleaded. 'For David's sake.'

'Oh God!' John exclaimed, and he stood up, lowered his head, like a man found guilty, and slunk in the direction of the house.

'You wait here, David,' Jacinta said. 'He'd be embarrassed if you were there.'

John went into the house. David and Jacinta waited for about ten minutes. Then Jacinta said, 'I think we should join them now.'

Batt took off his cap and shook hands with her.

'You're welcome to Knocklee,' he said. 'Would you like a cup of tea?'

'Yes. That would be nice.'

They spoke at length about the future. Batt and John were civil to each other as if they had never been at loggerheads. Jacinta pleaded with them to allow David to remain in Knocklee until the end of the summer holidays as she wanted to get some things done to the house to give David his own quarters where he could sleep and study. She would have everything ready for him when he returned just before the new school year began.

'But I want —,' David began.

'Leave it, Davy,' Batt interrupted. 'It will work out in time. We've come a long way today. We won't be rushing things now.'

✛ ✛ ✛

David told Josie of the arrangement when they were going to school in the bus next day.

'That means you won't be coming to this school next year,' Josie exclaimed.

'That's right. My dad will be booking me in to St Andrew's School in Cork. But I might be coming down here for the holidays and midterms. It has to be worked out yet. I'm just hoping.'

Josie turned and looked out the window. She kept looking out for a long time, as if she found the passing landscape of tremendous interest.

'Would you help me with something before I go?' David asked.

'What?' She turned back and looked at him. She had the serious look that came on her when she was bothered about something.

'I want to get to know everything about the place,' David said. 'I want to know all the plants and flowers, all their names, the birds, the animals, the butterflies, the insects – everything.'

'You'll have to get books,' Josie said, and her eyes brightened with enthusiasm. 'I know. We'll ask Dracula what books we should have and we might be able to get them in the town library.'

They found Dracula almost as eager as they were themselves. He gave them his own books on loan to help them to identify the plants and birds and insects, and he showed them how to press flowers. He gave them project exercise books with spaces for drawings and suggested that they draw pictures as well as they could of anything they could find and identify. They promised that they would show him the project when they had finished.

David and Josie began their study of the hill and glen. Samples of flowers and grasses, and crude drawings of birds and butterflies began to fill their notebooks. They were astonished at the variety of flowers on the hillside and along the glen floor. Flowers had been there always, but they hadn't bothered to look before. Now they could be seen bending down and admiring the delicate petals of wood sorrel, stitchwort, saxifrage, butterwort, or common vetch as if they had discovered precious gems.

To Ned and Batt they were just wild flowers. In the same way, birds were merely birds, but David and Josie saw the dipper, the grey wagtail, the kingfisher, the lark, and the meadow pipit, and what were merely crows or scald crows to the old folk became jackdaws, rooks, hooded crows, and ravens to the young

152

people. All the young Farrens had joined in the project and accompanied Josie and David on the slopes of the hills and along the glen.

As the month of August moved on, the whortleberries were ripe and they spent a few days gathering them in buckets and bringing them to the Farren house for Julie to make jam. Ned and Julie called them 'fraocháns' but the young ones called them by the name they found in the book, 'whortleberries'.

✝ ✝ ✝

A letter arrived from David's dad to say that he would come for him on the following Tuesday

'I want to leave the notebooks at home today,' David said when he called to Farrens' on Monday, the day before he was to leave.

'Why?' Josie asked. 'I thought we were going to look at the shore of the lake.'

'I know that,' David said, 'but I'll be leaving tomorrow and I want to go to the top of the hill, just to look at the whole place before I go.'

Josie and Lucy went with David. As they climbed up past Batt's house, Lucy forged ahead and Josie and David dawdled along, talking about the project.

'You can show it to Dracula when you go back in September,' David said. 'I'd like if you'd write to me to tell me what he said.'

'And if I write to you, will you write back to me?' Josie asked.

'I will of course. I was going to write to you anyway.'

They said nothing for a while, just walked along side by side in silence.

'Will you be going to the same school as Susan Branagan?' Josie asked.

'No,' David told her. 'She'll be in Xantia Academy for girls, and I'll be going to St Andrews. That's a boys' school.'

'But you'll be seeing her,' Josie said.

'Of course I will. She lives just three doors down from us.'

'I know,' Josie said.

'Why are you asking me about Susan Branagan?' David asked. 'She's the last thing on my mind at the moment.'

'What is on your mind at the moment?' Josie asked.

'This place. I want to get to the top of the hill and fill my eyes with it to carry it in my mind until I come back again.'

'Why?'

'Because it's my mom's place, and I think it's my place too. Anyway I've got used to it and I like it.'

At the top of the hill they looked down on the glen, pointing out all the spots they knew, as if they were looking at it in a picture. They looked to the north, the panorama of fields and hedges and dark evergreen plantations here and there. David checked the sheep. They were all grazing peacefully.

'We should be going down,' Lucy said. 'It will be getting dark soon.

'Just another few minutes,' David said. He wanted to linger. But the sun was dropping down to the west and they had to leave. Lucy had gone ahead and Josie and David followed, not speaking.

They came to a difficult place where they had to descend a face of bare rock with some loose stones. It had been easy to climb on the way up, but going down was hazardous; one could slip and tumble. Lucy had managed to scramble down and was gone ahead. David and Josie joined hands to help each other climb down. When they got down they didn't release hands, and they walked all the way down, hand in hand and silent.

'Are you not going in?' Josie asked as they passed Batt's house.

'I'll go down to the road with you,' David said. 'I won't be

154

seeing you for a while then.'

'The mid-term isn't far away,' Josie said.

'It's eight weeks,' David said.

When they reached the road, David released her hand, and she ran away without another word. As she passed Lucy, David could hear the younger girl say, 'What's wrong with you?'

David turned and walked back to the house.

29

Parting

John Lakes arrived at about two o'clock the following day. He parked the car at the other side of the rampart, then walked down to the house. Batt welcomed him and the two of them had friendly words for each other. David had already packed his bags. Batt had got him a new bag in Coombowler because he had collected a few personal items and they wouldn't all fit in the rucksack he brought with him when he came to Knocklee. It was time for David and Batt to say goodbye, but David knew Batt wouldn't say it, nothing so final.

'I'm getting the phone,' Batt blurted out.

'Good!' David said, and they spoke no other word.

They didn't shake hands, just stood and gave each other a long look. Then Batt nodded and David bent down and picked up his bags. He walked to the car and he didn't look back.

'Jacinta didn't come,' John told David. 'She said she would stay and have a meal ready for us to celebrate your homecoming.'

He took David's bags and put them in the boot.

The Farrens were out on the road when they were passing. They waved at David. They were all there – except Josie. David was disappointed. He looked back towards the house and he saw her, standing inside the gable window. He would write to her.

When the car reached the bend before the main road, David took in the whole glen in a quick glance, Murdons', Tim the Fiddler's, and Knocklee with its rocky face, the ribbon of smoke from the chimney, the tops of the birch trees at the west side of the house. Batt was standing on the rampart, gazing after the car as it rolled along the glen road. He stood there, alone and still as the gallaun in the haggard. David lowered the window and shouted at the top of his voice, 'I'll be back!'

If Batt heard his cry it could only have been a faint new note mingling with the ancient sounds of the countryside, larks singing, sheep bleating, and the soft sigh of the breeze in the birches, the muted music that had been a background to life in the glen for generations.

30

Psalm Twenty-Three:
A Psalm Of David

The Lord *is* my shepherd; I shall not want.

He maketh me to lie down in green pastures:
He leadeth me beside the still waters.

He restoreth my soul: He leadeth me in the paths
of righteousness for His name's sake.

Yea, though I walk through the valley of the
shadow of death, I will fear no evil: for Thou art
with me; Thy rod and Thy staff they comfort me.

Thou preparest a table before me in the presence of
mine enemies: Thou anointest my head with oil; my
cup runneth over.

Surely goodness and mercy shall follow me all the
days of my life; and I will dwell in the house of
the Lord forever.